A REBELLIOUS BREED

MISCELLANEOUS PAPERS

A REBELLIOUS BREED

A Nineteenth Century Tale of West Ham, East London

HAMILTON HAY

Matador
9 Priory Business Park
Kibworth Beauchamp
Leicestershire LE8 0RX, UK
Tel: (+44) 116 279 2299
Fax: (+44) 116 279 2277
Email: books@troubador.co.uk
Web: www.troubador.co.uk/matador

ISBN 978 1783060 498

British Library Cataloguing in Publication Data.
A catalogue record for this book is available from the British Library.

Typeset by Troubador Publishing Ltd, Leicester, UK
Printed and bound in the UK by TJ International, Padstow, Cornwall

Matador is an imprint of Troubador Publishing Ltd

Dedicated to the memory of
My Mother
born in Tidal Basin
and other ancestors from
the Borough of West Ham

An asterisk ★ indicates the name of a historical figure involved in the events described. Occasionally I have used actual words they used.

Contents

The Main Characters

The Waltons
James Walton
William James (Will), his son
Mary Badman, Will's companion
Frank, son of Will and Mary
Joe Badman, Mary's brother

The Horths
Frederick Horth
Jane, wife of Frederick
Emma, daughter of Frederick and Jane
Grace, daughter of Emma
Walter Horth, Frederick's brother

The Haigs
John Haig
Alfred, his son
Robert Haig, brother of John
Edward, son of Robert Haig

The Bradys
Shaun And Mairead Brady
Patrick and Marion Brady

And

Thirkankara Chandragupta, "Adi", the prince

Rise like lions after slumber
In your unvanquishable number–
Shake your chains to earth like dew
Which in sleep has fallen on you–
Ye are many – they are few.

PB Shelley, "The Mask of Anarchy"

To be in a passion you good may do
But no good if a passion is in you.

W Blake, "Auguries of Innocence"

CHAPTER ONE

The Uprooting

A six-year old boy was standing inside the doorway of his home when he heard squawking noises. He recognised the voices of chickens but this time they seemed to be screaming. Then just as suddenly, all went quiet. Next moment his dad appeared. The reason for the recent kerfuffle became apparent.

"Dad, why have you killed those two chickens?" he asked. "We can't get no more eggs now."

James's dad stood in front of his son. In each hand he was grasping a dead bird with its neck twisted. Blood dripped out of their mouths. His dad's face looked both drawn and tired. With a voice more upset than angry, he said, "Coz' we can't keep them any longer, not on the road. Now go and help your grandad and brother see if there's any more 'taters in the ground out back, or muck out the stable – just make yourself useful."

"Dad, John says we're leaving home. Is that true?" asked the boy.

"Later on this evening, we'll sit round together and we'll talk. But for now, don't stand around asking questions."

"Run along, James, there's a good boy." The voice was that of his mum. That day the locks of her auburn hair were dishevelled, her face worn and sad.

"Give me those birds, husband. I'll pluck 'em. At least we'll feed well tonight."

The boy stood there, confused.

"Go," shouted his dad.

"Don't be hard on him, dear. It's probably all a bit much for him at his age." Whenever there seemed to be a problem, mum smoothed things over just like she always did. James still stood there, tears filling his eyes. He loved his dad as well and didn't like to get on the wrong side of his temper. But he could tell dad was not really angry.

A gentle push from his mother and a soft "Go on, my love," and he hurried to the small piece of land at the back of the house. There he saw his elder brother John and their grandad scraping the ground. They were scavenging for any remaining vegetables or potatoes still left in the soil. John was doing most of the work. Poor grandad frequently stopped to dry his eyes. James had never seen his grandad cry before.

James tried to help but couldn't. His efforts to dig into the soil were half-hearted. John noticed this and said, "Go along and see to Cobbler – his straw will need mucking out. I'll join you soon." Even his brother's voice, he was fourteen now, seemed disturbed.

Once they had had two horses, now there was just this one. Cobbler was his best friend, after his mum and dad, brother and grandad. James loved to sink his head into the horse's soft mane. The horse was a handsome white colour, his nature warm and comforting. James often chattered away to the horse while rubbing down his friend. The horse seemed to understand everything he said.

Suddenly, a familiar voice called out. "Hello, James, you always were very fond of that horse." It was his Uncle John. "Ah, don't worry, I'll do my best to look after him for you."

"But it's my job. Cobbler doesn't need anybody else," said James.

"I think you need to come with me and talk to your dad," said Uncle John.

The boy ran to find his dad. "Dad, why is uncle talking about looking after our horse?"

Dad crouched down and put his face level with his son and said, "Because we can no longer afford to feed him. Your uncle has got a new job as a groom for Squire Eastwood. He will be responsible for a number of horses there. Cobbler will be well looked after, I promise."

At that moment, Uncle John appeared. He had put a rope round the horse's neck and was leading him away. "No," screamed the boy, "he can't have him." He rushed up to the horse, clutching the horse's foreleg. The horse lent his head down so the boy could sink his tears into that soft hair just one more time.

"Let go of Cobbler now James," said his father. "It's time to say goodbye."

"Can I come and see him?" asked the boy.

"Of course you can," replied Uncle John, "whenever you're in the area."

James did as he was told. Uncle John led the horse away, down the track that led away from their home. James's mother stood behind him. They stayed like that until his special friend had disappeared from view in the woods below.

That evening they sat outside on the ground. It had been a warm spring day. Grandad sat on the wooden chair made by his son, while James's mum perched on her spinning stool. The one person who could not sit down was James's dad. He was pacing up and down, getting more and more angry with every step he took.

"We know prices have hit the roof these last few years. But they'll come down again. And if we get work till at least this autumn, we'll get by. I say we should stay and fight. Not give in to these agents of Lord Haverleigh. They got no right to our land, any more than we have." Addressing grandad in particular he continued, "You and my mum have worked this land for many years. Why should you give it up and we all become homeless as a result? I know things are tough and there's not much money around and yes, Betsy's woollen goods don't sell so well. But people can see for themselves that her stuff is better than that cheap cotton stuff from up north."

"Folks hasn't got so much money to buy like they used to. They buy what they can afford," said mum.

"I'm still convinced we can survive, I'm sure of it."

All this time, Grandad had sat quietly in his chair, just looking at the ground.

"Son, you don't understand," he said quietly.

"We should get together with others and take on the landlord's men." James's dad continued to get more and more excited.

"Henry," James's mother shouted, "leave your dad alone, will you? Can't you see he's in just as bad a state as you? Getting angry won't get us anywhere."

Then in a soft voice, grandad turned to his son and said, "Listen, will you? These people say we can't prove title to this land – their papers show it belonging to the squire. It seems he wants to enlarge his estate to put livestock on these acres. I can't win. Besides, how can we earn enough these days? I'm old now – it's probably the workhouse for me unless the vestry helps me out. You and your family should stick together and do the best you can. It won't be easy for any of us. There's too many men as is looking for work. You might have to try something different. Stick together and you'll get by. Now leave me alone."

But grandad couldn't stop himself now. Words poured out of him. "Don't forget, I was born here in Rayleigh. Me and your late mother had many a good memory of being here. I'm a farmer. I live and breathe the land. My roots are here. No doubt soon I'll die here, though not on this smallholding. I can accept things better perhaps because I've had my best years – yours is to come. Whatever you get, you'll have to fight for it. Believe that somehow you can win. That's the point – knowing you're never going to get beat, whatever life throws at you. Now leave me be, I say."

James had never heard his grandad say so much. He was sure he would never forget what he'd heard, as long as he lived. At that moment in time grandad didn't look a broken man, but one who was very proud and a hero.

"Word is that the land agents will be arriving sometime tomorrow afternoon to clear all of us folk in this neck of the woods," said John.

"Then I suggest we prepare to leave in the morning so we don't have to meet them," replied dad. Silence implied all was agreed.

James had a restless night. He lay on the floor of the cottage, just as he always did, but that night things were different. Images of dead chickens hanging upside down by the door and of watching 'Cobbler' taken away filled his mind. He could not understand why they were leaving. Something important was about to happen. There was this fear that somebody was coming to take away his home and punish him and his family.

"Mum, I can't sleep," he whispered towards the corner where his mother was.

"Hush, James. Do the best you can and be a good boy."

He sensed that they were all awake and feeling as sad

as he was. But that night one thing he did feel was that at least the whole family would stay together. Mum was up early, bundling together their few possessions. But her spinning wheel she left inside the house. "Aren't you taking your spinning wheel with you?" James asked.

"No, my dear. I'm leaving that for old mother Truscott, in the dell. She'll drop in for it later today."

"How are you going to spin more wool for making clothes?" he asked.

"Don't worry my dear. I've got plenty of spun wool in those bags there. Besides, Mrs Truscott is only looking after it till the day I come back."

"Will that happen, mum?"

"I'm sure it will. We just have to be patient and wait and see."

He believed everything mum said was bound to happen and would come true. Meanwhile his dad and John were putting into the cart all they owned – clothing, blankets, spun wool, two chairs, pewter pot and a cooking stove. The plough was simply abandoned. Grandad closed the door of their home. He then stood there for a moment, not certain what to do.

"Come with us, for now. We're not going to just leave you here," said James's dad. Grandad sat in the cart and off they trundled, with dad harnessed up like Cobbler used to be and John at the back pushing. James walked alongside his mum. Everyone was consumed by the silence of their own thoughts.

They spent a month meandering about the area without any offers of work and living off the kindness of others. "You know, my dear," said James's dad to his wife, "Essex is such a pretty county to look at. There are plenty of woods, trees, rolling hills and fertile green land – it's just such a shame that there are too many people trying to be farm workers."

"All I keep seeing are notices saying, 'No Trespassers'" replied mum. "It all seems to be private land now."

Every day they would come across other cartloads of people. The lucky families still had a horse to pull them and their possessions. A few words might be exchanged like, "You know anywhere where there's work to be got, mister?" Replies would invariably be a "no".

"Landowners won't take on men from outside their area."

"Got any suggestions where we could try next?"

Mostly the answer was also "no", with nobody giving away any information, in case others got to find work before them. However one traveller was more helpful.

"I hear that around Ongar and Epping the soil is more fertile. With good crop rotation, vegetables and potatoes can be grown all year. It's in London where all the produce is wanted. The market at Whitechapel, near the City of London, is supposed to be huge."

"What's the wages like in the place you mentioned, mate?" asked James's dad.

"Rumour has it that the wages might be better by a bob or two than elsewhere."

James's dad thanked the man and their ways parted. While his mum and dad and grandad were talking about what to do next, James was full of excitement at the sound of a place called London. Whitechapel market would be fun, with lots of people and horses and fruit and vegetables. Only trouble was that thinking about food made him hungry. They had only eaten a few raw carrots that day, the gift of a kind couple they had passed earlier.

Meanwhile the adults had decided it was time to go further afield and try the Ongar area. But grandad did not want to go back on the road. "Drop me off here. We're not too far away from Rayleigh. I'll make my own way to the workhouse there and don't try to stop me. You'll have one less mouth to feed."

Grandad was hugged by all the family in turn. James's dad had a hard time not crying. He was very reluctant to let go of his own dad in these circumstances. "I only hope I can live to be as good a father to my family as you have been to us," he said. As they moved off without grandad, James kept turning back to see if grandad was still there. He noticed grandad had not moved from the spot where they had left him. James waved one last time before his view was obstructed by a turn in the road.

The family tried their luck in various places and they managed to get by on casual work but as the seasons moved from summer to autumn, they knew that come November, their chances of farmwork would be even less. A new approach was needed.

"I've got an idea," said James's dad one day. "Since there's all these crops being carted backwards and forwards to London, why don't I try and become a waggoner and make 'em?"

"You've always been a bit handy with wood, making tables and chairs and such like," said mum encouragingly. "Let's ask around if there's a waggoner's yard somewhere round here."

That was how they ended up in Abridge. Dad was taken on, to see if he could learn the trade. Meanwhile the family managed to find a room in a farm outbuilding in Lambourne where they could stay. Dad proved to be skilful and the firm was doing well. With the population living in London getting larger, wagons and carts were needed in ever greater numbers. They also made fancy carriages for the gentry. Dad was happy and regular money was coming in at last. James loved to hear his dad come back from work. Talk of the wagonloads passing through on their way to the City of London still excited his imagination.

"Seeing all these supplies, makes you think about all those very hungry people back home who could do with some of this food but ain't got the money to pay for it." These words passed Dad's lips more than once. It reminded all of them of the fact that they had known what it was to be hungry as well.

One day James's dad announced he was taking a day off to go back to Rayleigh to see how his father was.

"He looked old and frail" said dad when he returned. "The workhouse master doesn't ask too much of him apart from a bit of gardening around the houses of one or two of the local gentry. But your grandad has slowed down a lot and he doesn't eat much. He complained to me that after having lived off good country food for much of his life, he did not take kindly to the slops they served up at the workhouse."

James's dad turned to his family and said sadly, "It will only take a cold chill in the coming winter for dad to be blown away with pneumonia. When we said goodbye to each other I think both of us knew we would not see each other again, alive that is."

For a few years life for James seemed more settled. Although John and even James got occasional farm work, it was their dad's wages that kept them going for the moment. One day mum told the brothers she was going to have a baby. "I do hope it's the baby girl I've been wanting for a long time." John and James were excited as well. The thought of having a baby sister would be fun.

At the time the family was sitting down to a meal which consisted of just potato soup and a slice of bread. "Husband, the cost of everything's going sky-high, especially the bread, tea and coal. I'm afraid this is all we can afford. I must keep knitting. We need any money we can get."

"Betsy, you're no spring chicken. I don't want you overworking and taking chances with the baby," said dad. "You're already looking a bit tired, what with the cold weather we've been having. Please, my dear, don't overdo it."

Just look at the state of our clothes and that of our kids," replied mum. "Our clothes are threadbare. We're all cold and we have less to eat. I've got to do something to keep us all alive."

Once a few articles were ready, she would go traipsing along the road between Lambourne and Ongar to try and sell her wares at the market. She was wearing herself out and her family knew it.

One day she set off for the market and didn't come back. When dad arrived back home that evening, his immediate response was to set off back along the road to Ongar to look for her. He soon came back. "It's too dark. I'll never find her. Tomorrow I'm going to go all the way to Ongar and I won't come back until I've found mother." James begged his dad to take him with him.

Next day they were about to set off early when John announced, "I'm not coming with you. I want to go to Sheering. A number of us are gathering there to protest about food prices and no work," he said.

His father was immediately alarmed by this. "Avoid trouble, for mother's sake as well as mine." To calm his father John said, "Yes, ok, I'll be careful."

James and his father got to Ongar and searched all over the town centre and the market area. The square was bustling with the cries of the traders. Everywhere was the chatter of the people while dogs wandered about demolishing any scraps that came their way. James had never seen anything like it before. Meanwhile his dad was asking people whether they had seen anybody looking like James's mother. Though one or two knew of the person James's dad described, nobody knew of her whereabouts. Somebody suggested speaking to the beadle. Dad and James wandered up and down the stalls until they found him. They asked for his help.

"A woman such as you describe was found yesterday by a local gentleman. We did not know who she was. It would be helpful if you came with me to the parish hall where we have laid her body. We was hoping that someone would soon come and identify her before we have to bury her ourselves."

Hoping against hope that the beadle had not been talking about his wife, but anxious at the same time to find her, dad and James went to the parish hall. They were met by a kindly lady who led them in. In one corner there was a body, having already been placed in a rough wooden coffin, the kind quickly assembled by the undertaker for a pauper.

James stood back, almost hiding behind his father as the lid of the coffin was lifted. Immediately, father covered his face and in a voice muffled by emotion said, "That's her, that's my wife."

James could not resist wanting to take a peek at his mother again. What he saw surprised him. His mother's face had such a peaceful expression. "Is that what you look like, when you're dead?" But it was all too much for him and he burst into tears. Father put his arm round his son.

13

James's gaze then turned to look around the room. To his surprise, he saw a small bundle in another makeshift box in a corner. He felt he had to go and have a look at what was inside. Shocked, he called out, "It's a baby. I think she's alive. Is it mother's, dad?" he said.

The beadle stepped in, "Yes, it belongs to your mother, God rest her soul."

Turning to the father, the beadle continued, "This good woman you met at the doorway has been trying to wet nurse it as best she could. We were expecting someone to come forward to claim the baby soon or it would surely die."

"How did all this happen, officer?" asked dad.

"Well, sir, your wife was found on the road to Ongar where she had collapsed. A gentleman driving his carriage saw her lying by the track. He acted the Good Samaritan, picked her up and drove her to a doctor in Ongar. Crying and in great pain, she gave birth in his surgery. Then I'm afraid, she gave up the ghost and died."

"One more thing to say, if it will comfort you," the beadle said, "I was told by the infirmary that your wife, before she died, had been told it was a girl. Asked what name she wanted to give the child, she had whispered Sarah."

With another shake of his head, the beadle added, "but we are fearful the little one is not going to survive."

The kind man who had taken mother to Ongar had kept in touch with the doctor. He offered to help take the body, the baby, James and his dad back to their home in his carriage. For James it was as though the journey would never end. Two hours of total silence. When finally they got back to Lambourne and had unloaded the carriage, the gentleman turned the horse round and quietly departed. He knew that dad had no money to pay him, nor was it expected.

Dad turned to James and said, "Remember this – not all of them gentry are cruel and heartless. There are good people, people with a heart among them, just as there are among the poor."

Soon after, Sarah died, starved of her mother's milk. She was buried alongside her mother. The local vicar suggested the words for a headstone:

> "In Memory of Betsy Walton 1786-1830,
> wife of Henry Walton and of their daughter
> Sarah who lived for 10 days
>
> In the name of the Father, here we plead
> This mother and child, your love receive."

While dad moved about the house like a damp rag, James sat outside and cried. He had now lost his mother and a baby sister. Without mother, he felt lonely and helpless. He was deeply unhappy. Memories came back of the other losses he had already suffered – the loss of his first home, 'Cobbler' his horse and his grandad. But this latest loss was the worst of all. His mother was the one person who made him feel happy and secure. She was the only one who could calm his fears. It was all wrong. Why were they so hard done by? Life was not fair.

But worse was to come. His brother John had not come back from Sheering. Dad found out that a few men had been arrested following unrest in the town and that the prisoners were being held prisoner in a new gaol at Colchester.

CHAPTER 2

We broke no law

"Please make your way up the stairs to the public gallery."
The guard had just opened the doors of the court house.
A number of bedraggled folk, worn down by their
journeys on foot from all parts of Essex, filed past and up
the steps as instructed.

They sat down on wooden benches in the public
gallery at the back looking down into the court. They
were there to bear witness to the fate of their friends and
relatives. This day would have a severe effect on their
lives, as well as the accused. Some were there for the Mile
End prosecution, others for the Sheering case. The court
would not be in session for an hour or so but people
resigned themselves to sit quietly and wait. Among the
public were James and his dad. They wanted to find out
whether John was among those on trial that day.

From their seats at the back, they had a good view of
the layout of the court. It was a stark and forbidding place
of dark wooden panels and seats, lit by only two small

windows. Being a damp day in December, the atmosphere was already one of gloom and despondency before the process of justice had even started. Around two elevated balconies were some seats with cushions for the gentry and their ladies. At ground level, on the right-hand side were the seats for the twelve jurors, on the left the benches for the lawyers and court officials. Next to them and near the judge, was the box where the witnesses would give their testimony. In the centre was a boxed area for the accused with steps which led down to the cells below. Dominating everything else was the judge's seat. It had a high red leather back, surmounted by the Royal Coat of Arms.

The Mile End trial went first. It resulted in heavy prison sentences for those charged and then convicted. It was all over rather rapidly. The verdict, "Guilty of Riotous Assembly", resulted in the ten men being put in prison for hard labour for between three and twelve months. The Court then adjourned and everybody had to rise for his Lordship to leave.

"Tis a bit harsh," said the man next to dad, "but I reckon that's because Mile End is too near the City of London. The city fathers must have taken fright and wanted 'em dealt with severely."

"Do yer know any of those who've been done?" asked dad.

"Several of them are mates of mine. Loads of us were there but those fellas were the unlucky ones who got arrested," replied the other man.

"How quickly do you think the other case – the Sheering one – will start?" asked Dad.

"Not yet. They won't come back until his Lordship, the jurors and the ladies have had a nice, leisurely lunch. Give it an hour or two, I'd say."

A sign that things were about to restart came when the jurors reappeared and the ladies took their places on the side balconies. Then came the dramatic moment when the prisoners made their appearance. One by one they climbed up the steps into their box, before turning to face the judge's seat. For a brief period they had the chance to turn round and view the public gallery. James's dad hung his head in his hands in a gesture of despair while James recognised his elder brother and gasped. The hair on his head had been shorn, like a sheep's. So had the hair of all the prisoners, but looking at his own brother, it seemed all wrong. As for the prisoners, there was an air of quiet resignation on all their faces as if they already understood that in the eyes of the law, they were already condemned.

The voice of the usher of the court boomed out, "All rise to receive His Lordship, Mr Justice Latimer."

The usher read out the charges. "George Burls, Shadrack Graves, Joseph Norris, David Thomas, Daniel Thomas, Richard Thomas, John Walton, you are each charged that on the 12th November 1830 in the village of Sheering you were acting in a riotous manner after being ordered to disperse by order of the law, and of resisting arrest by members of the militia, acting on the orders of their commander. How do you plead?" They all answered, "Not guilty," except Joseph Norris, who perhaps was calculating if he was going to get 'done' anyway, maybe he would get a lighter sentence by pleading guilty.

The main witness was Reverend Clarkson in whose parish the event took place. He was asked to describe what happened that day in the village of Sheering.

"It was around 11o'clock that I became aware of a crowd of around fifty to sixty labourers walking towards my residence," began the Reverend. "I decided I would go out and meet them. Being a Reverend, that made me feel safe." These words produced smiles and a few quiet laughs among the attending gentry.

"I demanded of them their purpose in trespassing on my land. Being a rough-looking lot, I could only look around for someone to answer my question. The vast number of the men were unknown to me and I wondered why on earth they were interfering in my affairs when they had no business to. One man – I am convinced it was the man in the dock who goes by the name of George Burls – stated that the men were there to demand better wages. He wanted to explain how hard living was at present and how they had families to feed – that sort of thing. I told the crowd that that was nothing to do with me. Any talk of work and pay should be addressed to their own employers. I requested that they leave my land. I insisted they leave the village of Sheering in peace and go back home to their work. They were not welcome here.

"After some few minutes, the men realised I would have no truck with them. They turned their backs and walked away. I took note of their faces as best I could, in case I might need to prosecute any of them in the future in my capacity as a magistrate.

"Unfortunately, the crowd did not go away as instructed but drifted towards the village. They broke into smaller groups, going round the houses of the inhabitants demanding food, beer or money. The residents were clearly becoming frightened for their safety. I found this out when a gentleman farmer came up to my house that afternoon, insisting that something should be done about the situation and quickly.

"So I ordered my steward to assemble the men and I told them that I was requiring them to act as the local militia. Whilst not being armed, I conferred on them the power to arrest anyone who resisted my orders to disperse. My steward alone I allowed to carry a shotgun.

"Within minutes we reached the centre of the mob. Unruly behaviour was apparent and some of the crowd may have been drinking. I stood on the steps outside the local grocer's store and ordered the crowd to disperse. They failed to do so; I therefore ordered the militia to arrest a few of them. There was some resistance and some scuffling took place. My steward made noticeable his weapon which calmed things down. The militia arrested seven men who I thought seemed to be leading the riot.

"That seemed to have the effect of making the crowd more subdued. The man in the dock, Burls, told the crowd they had better go now and not get themselves into further trouble. They seemed to listen to him and the men drifted away. I next ordered the militia and my steward to accompany the prisoners to the gaol in Harlow."

"Would you please tell the court what happened the next day?" asked the prosecutor.

"The next morning the prisoners were brought before me as the local magistrate. The prisoners were formally charged before being sent to the gaol here in Colchester."

The Reverend was duly thanked for his testimony. The prosecution's next witness was the steward, Barrett. His role was to confirm the identity of those charged but he seemed somewhat overawed by the proceedings.

"Are the accused in the dock the same as the men who came to Sheering that day?" asked the prosecutor.

"I can't say as how I rightly remember their faces, your honour," he stumbled

"You helped arrest them, did you not?"

"Yes, but there were lots of people around that day. We did what we were told to do." He was clearly unsure what to say, so the Judge stepped in.

"Can you confirm that you were there in Sheering on the 12th November when a large crowd had assembled?"

"Yes, your honour", replied Barrett.

"Good. The Reverend has already established that things could have got further out of hand if it had not been for the presence of the militia. Did you help to arrest the men who the Reverend believed were the ringleaders of the trouble taking place?"

"Yes, your honour."

"The men arrested that day are the same as those in the dock. Is that correct?"

"Perhaps, your Lordship," replied the steward.

"I must have a firmer answer than that. It is a simple question."

The steward was still hesitant.

"Come, my man, we can't be here all day. Were the accused there the day of the trouble in Sheering?" The judge's voice displayed all the force and authority he considered required to get Barrett to submit to his questioning.

The steward uttered a quiet "yes" which the judge insisted on him repeating louder. In the end Barrett answered firmly enough to be dismissed as a witness. His role had been satisfied in that he had been made to identify all of the prisoners as 'responsible for the riotous assembly' and therefore guilty in the eyes of the court.

The Judge seemed to think there was no need for further evidence. He therefore addressed the men to ask if they had anything to say in their defence. George Burls, a couple of years older than the others, spoke up, saying, "We have violated no law. We have injured no man and no property. We were acting together to preserve ourselves, our wives and children from degradation and starvation. We challenge all statements to the effect that we were causing a riot. We were peaceable. And we did not resist arrest. We could not figure out why some of us were being picked on. I repeat we are good citizens and we did not break any law."

The Judge then turned to the Jury. "Members of the Jury, there are two charges on the charge sheet. That of resisting arrest, I am prepared to forgo. The fact that the Reverend Clarkson had the presence of mind to arm his steward with a shotgun had a sufficient effect to cause the accused to submit to their arrest without any physical attack being made on the militia seeking to carry out their orders. So I am recommending that this charge be omitted from your deliberations.

"However the most serious charge is that of being party to a riotous assembly in the village of Sheering. You have all heard Reverend Clarkson's evidence which described the events of the day and the reason why the militia had to be called out. You have heard the testimony of the steward, Mr Barrett, whereby each of those standing in the dock was clearly identified as being present and therefore involved in the disturbance which took place. I would now ask you to consider your verdict."

As he concluded, the chief foreman sitting nearest to the Judge turned round in his seat to face his fellow jurors. A few nods and murmurs of guilty were exchanged among them – it was all over in seconds. Being asked for their verdict, the chief foreman replied, "Guilty" as each of the prisoner's names was read.

The Judge then addressed the convicted and asked if they had anything further to say before sentence was passed. George Burls stood up for the youngest of the prisoners, Daniel.

"This lad here, M'lord, is under sixteen. He was only

there that day to be with his brothers. He never said a word in anger; he caused no trouble but stayed by his brother's side. He's a good lad, works well when he has the chance. I would beg your honour to be kind to him and if possible, let him go free and be spared a criminal record against his name."

Without any further reflection, his lordship pronounced his judgement. "George Burls, it seems to me you were the main instigator of the troubles that day. For involvement in the riotous assembly at Sheering, I sentence you to eight months hard labour. Shadrack Graves, David, Daniel and Richard Thomas, John Walton – I sentence you to six months hard labour. Joseph Norris – I sentence you to three months hard labour. Case dismissed."

Silently, the men were led away. That day in court was to haunt James for the rest of his life.

Six months later, a shadowy figure emerged from the darkness at the back of the lodgings in Lambourne. A light had gone on inside and that had been the signal for the person to move. Looking nervously in every direction, he made his way round to the front door. He tapped quietly and waited till a man came to the door. They recognised each other instantly.

"John, you're home." Dad gave John a warm and firm embrace. "Welcome back, son." Within seconds James came running into the yard, saw John and hugged his brother. "I've been out in the fields, great to see you."

"Have you just been released?" asked dad.

"I was let out a few days ago but I've only been travelling by night and hiding in hedges and ditches in daytime so as no one could see me. With my shaved head, I didn't want to be recognised as a criminal. Where's mum?"

"Son, I'm sorry to tell you she died on the same day that you were being arrested."

For some minutes there was silence. James made a cup of tea. Then they all sat down while dad recounted the sad story. The death of the baby disturbed John as much as that of his mother. "The baby never had a chance. Life's cruel!"

"What was prison like, John?" asked James.

"Nothing but toil and misery from start to finish. Most of the time we were smashing rocks to break them up. The other unpleasant job was oakum picking. There seemed to be an endless supply of old ropes which had been used for all the dirtiest and filthiest tasks on ships. Unpicking the threads tore your fingers to shreds. None of the work made any sense. Then of course, each and every day we had to drag the chains around our feet which made every step difficult and painful. The guards went out of their way to make you feel like animals, without any dignity. We hated them. The only time I ever said 'thank you' to a guard was when finally he removed the chains off my ankles."

"What about that young lad who was convicted with you?" asked dad.

"Oh, Daniel. I think they broke his spirit completely,"

said John. "We've all been affected by our time there, knowing it would be hard to live normally again, but it was worse for him. Bastards."

For the next few days John laid low, allowing the two others to look after him. During the evenings, they talked further. Dad was enthusiastic about working in the coach-building business. When John asked James what he got up to, James said, "Now and again, I get odd pieces of work as a farm labourer, but I'm not keen about working on the land. I want to try something else but not sure what yet."

"I want to be a farmer alright," said John, "but nobody is going to give me a job in England with my criminal record."

His dad asked, "So what are you going to do next?"

"I've already made up my mind. It may come as a shock, but I'm going to emigrate. Not to Australia or Tasmania where those who are transported are sent. No, I want somewhere where I can walk free and be proud again. Be my own person – work the land and hopefully start a family. I'm going to Canada."

"Isn't that a bit risky?" asked his dad.

"I don't know, but I have nothing to lose," replied John. "I heard from other prisoners who were planning to do the same that large areas in the interior would be opening up soon. I'm hoping there will be opportunities for men like me to get some land and farm it."

"Canada is certainly a country for pioneers," remarked his Dad. "Just surviving will be tough. But you're young and I can see you've obviously been thinking hard about this for the past few months. But I shall miss you, son."

"Just give me time to look normal again, with my hair and general appearance," said John, "then I'll be off. I need to somehow work my way to Liverpool where the sailings to North America take place."

Dad let out a deep sigh. He was seeing his family falling apart around him. But he knew what he had to do when his son was finally ready to leave.

A week later, John left. Dad thrust five pounds into his hands. "Here's a few pounds which I've managed to save. Take it and use it wisely."

James kept quiet about the fact that the money was supposed to be towards the rent on their room and winter fuel bills.

They all knew they would be unlikely to be together again. For James it was yet another loss in his life. Anger was starting to build up inside him. He wanted to get back at all those who had made him and his family suffer. He could not as yet identify his enemies.

CHAPTER THREE

Essex Burns

"You ought to come and work with me," suggested dad to James. "It'll be a darn sight more regular in the way of money than scraping a few pennies together now and again from casual work on the land. I'll mention you to my gaffer."

Even as his dad said it, James felt uncertain whether coach building was the answer for him. Not that farm work was any better. Getting any work meant traipsing for miles each day in different directions in the hope of finding a farmer who on a daily basis wanted some job done – from sowing to harvesting, from digging up potatoes (which reminded him of the day when he had lost his home) to mucking out stables. One thing James had learnt by now was that employment on the land had changed for good. There were no longer any secure jobs on farms.

His dad came back from work the next day saying, "Great news, the gaffer agreed to take you on for a trial period. I'll have to get busy right away showing you how to use the various tools we use in the workshop. I'm sure you'll find it as worthwhile as I do. Just think, you help construct a cart or even a fancy carriage. The evidence is there for all to see for years to come."

"Yes, dad, I'll give it a go," said his son. "After all," he said to himself, "there's not much else going for me at the moment."

James had to admit that the workshop was an amazing place. The implements were so specialised. His dad told him about each of them, as well as introducing his workmates. They were a quiet lot who simply got on with whatever was being constructed at the time. The more skilled got to work on the axles, suspension and wheels, others the framework or shafts. Whilst carts were the vehicles they mostly made, now and again there were the 'specials' such as the fancy phaeton carriages which had just come into fashion. Some of the landowners were doing well and what better way of showing off your wealth than by driving round in some fancy two-wheeled carriage.

It was good and interesting work for the coach builders as newly-designed springs and spindles and an elliptical suspension system made the ride smoother and more stable. In addition, wheels and axles were improved. They had fancy doors, comfortable seats and folding hoods designed to keep the driver and his passengers dry during wet weather. The wood selected for the work was of a better quality and was a pleasure to handle and shape, dad said.

But while these men worked together sharing their love of their work, James felt like an outsider. He did his bit, learnt a lot about levelling and shaping wood and how to create joints of various kinds, but he did not like the routine of working, day in and day out, in one place. He couldn't settle down to regular work. His dad noticed this but said, "Your problem is that you've been idle for too long. Get a grip, lad."

"Dad, I'm no good at woodwork. I don't have your skill," said James.

"Then learn and stop moaning," was his dad's unsympathetic reply.

His dad began to feel his son was either deliberately clumsy or was he really useless? "You're making a right mess of things. You don't have to plane wood so heavily to get it level. You waste wood the way you work and it's still not right. I'm worried the foreman will want to get rid of you. It's only a small business – no room for someone who can't pull his weight."

If he'd been honest with his dad, James would have admitted that his mind was not on what he did by day. He looked forward to the evenings which he spent in east London, meeting shady characters from the underworld who could supply anything you could want, legal or not. Making deals and handling stolen property was much more fun than working in a timber yard.

It was a relief to James when one evening his dad said to him, "the gaffer told me to tell you that you're no longer wanted at the yard." James had a hard job looking upset.

"Then I'll try something else," said James, shrugging his shoulders. By this time his plans were well laid.

★

"We are very glad to hear you have plentiful crops and we hear that you have had the masheen[sic] to thrash some of it but we will give you warning if you have it again for as shure[sic] as you are a man alive next time that you have it you shall have a light. Another thing we hear is that you have had other parish men to do your harvest and that there is some wanting for work in your own parish. It would be well for you to discharge them for if you set them into your barn you shall have light: we don't wish to harm you if you employ your own people and thrash your corn by flail."

James Walton looked at the text. He had had a hand in helping the farm workers to write it. He had been making it his business to tour round the villages, trying to judge the amount of anger and hostility that was felt in each place he visited.

He nodded his approval before passing the script to the next man. Each man looked at, but did not necessarily read the text. They pretended to do so but those present knew who could and who couldn't read. "Have you thought about how you are going to deliver the letter?" asked James.

"My sister works at the manor house as a parlour maid," said one. "I'll get her to drop it on the floor in the hallway and wait for it to be found by the house-keeper. And before any of yous say it, yes, I'll tell her to be careful not to be seen handling or dropping it."

"If you're interested," said James, "I can supply you with some special matches, should you reckon you're likely to want them – if the letter doesn't do the trick."

One of the group leaned forward, eyeing James closely. "Who are you and what's so special about these matches?" he asked.

"Well, first of all, I'm a farm worker like you. Down my way in Abridge, they're getting ready to take action like you. Anyway, I came to see how you were going about things round here. As for these matches, they're made of sulphur. They ignite quickly and easily, so no messing around with tinder boxes, hoping they give off enough of a spark. These matches are easy to hide under one's clothing which makes them ideal for the job of setting light to a barn and moving quickly away so as not to be caught."

"Have these matches got a name?" asked someone.

"Lucifer Matches," replied James.

"Can you get hold of some for us?"

"Sure. I can do that. I know the bloke who makes them down Whitechapel way. It will cost you a bob or two mind. Not a lot though, considering their usefulness and reliability."

"If we want any, how do we get hold of you?" asked another member of the group.

"That's easy. I'll be around the area again pretty soon. I'll have some with me," replied James.

That was agreed, so James left. Once outside, a smile came over his face. If he could manage to sell some matches here, they might well be used on the estates of that reverend who had been responsible for putting away his brother John.

As James made his way back home, he felt very pleased with himself. He could foresee a way to earn himself some useful cash by turning the current situation to his advantage. Farm workers throughout Essex had had enough and were ready to take some form of violent action. They felt betrayed by their landlords for taking away work at harvest time by using threshing machines. They were angry that wages were kept low by their masters. Only profits mattered nowadays. It was this anger that James wanted to exploit.

He would be opposing the landowners in his own way. Burning crops and harvests would hurt the landowners where it mattered most – in their pockets. "The workers will do the burning," he said to himself, "all I've got to do is supply the matches. I just have to be careful not to get caught handling them."

His cheerful mood lasted as far as the courtyard at the back of the farmstead in Lambourne where he and his dad still lived. Before he reached the door, James saw his dad standing there outside. Advancing towards James, his father sputtered out the words, "What have you been up to, you rogue?"

"What's up dad?" replied James. "What are you talking about? I've been out trying to find some work."

"Don't come that with me, you and your slippery tongue. I've got Tom Camp inside with his young girl, Eliza. She's pregnant and her dad has got her to confess that you're the father."

"How does she know?" asked James.

"Eliza says you went with her into the fields this summer. She didn't go with anyone else," replied dad.

"Well, what am I supposed to do about it then?"

"You've got no choice," said dad. "He insists you marry his daughter to avoid any disgrace in his family and you know Tom Camp – he won't take 'no' for an answer. Fine mess you've got us into. She'll have to stay here with us, and you, my son, will have to look after her and the child."

"What do you want me to do now, dad?"

"Go inside, say you're sorry for what's happened but say you'll do what's best for Eliza."

So in went James for his roasting by Tom. Once his anger had been assuaged by James agreeing to accept his responsibility, Tom calmed down. But he insisted on a proper church wedding. Eliza, meanwhile, never said a word.

In church, on the day of the wedding, Tom Camp seemed reluctant to sign the marriage certificate. James imagined it was because he was unhappy at things. But it turned out it was because he couldn't write his name so the vicar got him to sign it by placing a mark – just a dot – on the document.

Once Eliza came and lived in their home, dad seemed happier. Pleased to have a woman around the place again, his good humour led him to tell his son what had been a little family secret. "I did the same as you years ago. I got your mother pregnant but her father didn't create the same fuss as Tom Camp. There were so many mouths to feed in her family and they only had a tiny parcel of land. Your mother's father said to me, 'If you can feed her, yer can 'ave 'er. The one difference between us then and you and Eliza today was that your mother and I never got married."

By 1845, there were outbreaks of rick burning all over the county. James had been busy. He'd be going down to Whitechapel to purchase his stock of matches. These he would stow in an old suitcase which he kept hidden in Hainault Forest. Some of the supply he would carry in an old leather bag and then go off to deliver them to those who had requested the matches. As far as Eliza was concerned he would appear to be going off to find work. Eliza never asked him what or where he was going. She noticed that the state of his clothes and shoes didn't look as though they'd been wading through fields and mud all day. She also knew he liked to drink so she assumed he was with his mates in the Bald-faced Stag. But she had to admit he did seem to be earning some money.

It was down at the pub that James found out best what was being reported regarding the location of the fires which he had helped create. One or two of those in the pub had a shrewd idea what James was up to but pretended they didn't.

"I hear there was some rick-burning in Sheering," one mate said.

"D'you know on whose estate?" asked James. Nobody knew, but James quietly hoped it was the one owned by the family of the man who had sent his brother John to jail. But it was a kind of revenge, something to let that village know that workers could and would strike back if their faces were pushed hard enough into the ground.

"Did you hear about that fire up Tendering way?" a close mate, Jack, asked. "It was at night of course. The fire had already burnt down one barn before the landowner rushed out in his nightshirt, shouting for everybody to get busy putting out the flames. But there were not enough buckets and the fire was still out of control. The village fire engine was sent for but when it arrived on the scene, it was found someone had cut the hose so it was useless. I'm told they didn't like the bugger so they couldn't care a dam about his harvest."

"But what about people getting trapped inside a building?" said another.

"That's different. Where people's lives are concerned, everybody joins in to get them out," said James.

"S'not the same with animals though," said one. "I heard that another blaze spread to a pig- sty. Nobody tried to get the pigs out alive. Poor creatures died squealing horribly. But when people reckoned no one was looking they scavenged among the ruins to help themselves to some nice mouthfuls of well-smoked ham."

"Best meal they'd probably had in months," said another.

"You get around a bit, James. How do the locals react when they see a fire? Are they glad or sad to see crops going up in smoke?" said Jack.

"As I've seen it, and like Jack says, often the fires are welcomed as a chance to get back at unpopular landowners," said James. "But I tell you one thing. After a fire has taken place, everybody lies low waiting for the landowner's reaction. Usually the farmers can't believe how anyone could be so nasty to them." His audience laughed.

"Then they start the blame game. They want to know who was responsible. 'Course nobody owns up. The landowner persists, so people blame outsiders – anyone will do – tinkers, vagrants and Irish navvies – to put them off the scent.

"Next, notices start to go up. Huge rewards are offered for information as to the identities of the incendiaries and such like. But do you know, I've actually seen one notice which mentioned the sum of a thousand pounds as a reward."

"Blimey, that's more than any of us could earn in a lifetime!" said one.

"But it doesn't work," said James. "People say nothing. No one snitches on another. Only thing you can't prevent perhaps is someone wanting to point the finger at somebody else to settle some private grievance."

Then came the day when James was in the pub and a mate rushed through the door. "They're coming for you

James," he said. "Some bloke has named you as being responsible for a fire in Loughton?"

"Do I know him?" asked James.

"I don't know. What does that matter? You'll have to hide quickly. Ask Sam Tomes over there if he will hide you in his outbuilding."

"OK," said Sam, "come with me." They set off for this hideout. It was the upper storey of a barn which was reached by a ladder. James climbed the ladder then pulled it up and hid himself and the ladder among some straw. But after a few hours, Sam came back.

"You'll have to scarper," he said. "The constables have already been to your house and the pub, looking for you. It won't be long before they trace you here."

Immediately James jumped down, thanked Sam and gave him a couple of quid to keep quiet. He made a beeline for the road out of the village. His route seemed obvious – towards London. There he would lie low for a while.

Moving at speed, travelling by night and hiding by day, he got out of Essex into Middlesex. He needed somewhere to stay where nobody knew him. He decided to head out for one of those new suburbs being built outside London, in Islington. It would be an ideal place from his point of view. It was near the City of London and the London markets, yet far enough away to conceal himself should any trouble be brewing.

He had to face the fact that he was now an outlaw. The authorities would be out to get him. He couldn't bring down any of them but he was sure going to take what he could from the upper classes. He wanted revenge on all those who he considered had made his life so far into a series of personal disasters. Hadn't his mum died because she was worn out by hardship? Hadn't grandad been pushed into the workhouse? Hadn't they all known hunger? Hadn't his brother John been trying to stand up for farmworkers and been punished for his nerve in doing so? The system was rotten.

"I couldn't beat the system but I could try to hurt it and survive at the same time," he said to himself. "I wouldn't go around begging anyone for favours. Looks as though I will have to accept being a criminal from now on and stealing is the obvious way to get at the rich."

He realized he would have to be careful who he could trust. He would have to be constantly vigilant. If he were caught, it would mean either a death sentence or transportation for life.

CHAPTER 4

Evading Responsibilities

James Walton decided it was time to adopt a new front. He would no longer pretend to look like a farm labourer but the kind of man you could do business with, a charming, snappy dresser maybe, a man of the world and that sort of thing. He would be amiable, cheerful, a good bloke to discuss 'business' with down the pub. With a pose like that, he would keep his protective shell around him. He would use other people for his own purposes. He would become sly and cunning whilst giving off the appearance of being the opposite.

James felt things were going well. Finsbury was an ideal location for getting into Whitechapel where the underworld thrived. Meanwhile Essex and the forest were excellent places to hide or store items or trade in poached goods. He would always carry a good supply of cash. All his clothes had hidden pockets where money could be accessed if needed. Cash could get you anything you wanted.

He found a new girl – Susanna. They seemed made for each other. She liked fun and was care-free. She offered him a chance to forget the past and to indulge in sex. It was no surprise when Susanna got pregnant. Their first child was a son they called Harry.

Their first lodging was in a small courtyard of apartments in Bride Street, near Liverpool Road. It was part of a new small block of houses which at first had no water or drainage pipes. After Harry was born they moved into another place in the street, part of another development. In spite of houses going up everywhere on what had been open farmland, their house looked out over open land. Only one tall building was visible in the distance– it was Pentonville Prison, which made James a little nervous.

One nagging worry remained in James's mind – what had become of his dad? He had tried to send a letter to Lambourne with one of the new postage stamps but he had never had a reply. He had also tried sending notes by means of contacts back in Essex, but got nowhere. Then out of the blue, James received a letter from his wife Eliza dated October 1852.

"Dear James

I found your address after looking through your father's possessions. There I found the letter you had sent him earlier this year.

I have to inform you that your father died recently. He was so upset when he heard you had run away to

London. He was also informed of what you had been doing supplying matches for burning farm buildings. He went downhill rapidly after that. He was all alone. He began blaming himself for everything that had gone wrong with his family – one son falsely convicted of a crime and gone abroad, the other turning out to be a real criminal who had run away. And he had not been a good husband or done enough for his wife Betsy, or so he thought. Poor man – how unhappy he was. He stopped eating, neglected himself and just wanted to die. I believe he tried to get sick. Then he caught a chill and died a few weeks later.

I have more bad news for you. My Father came and took me and our daughter Joan home. He got so angry at what you had done. He said you were not fit to live. You know how strong his religious ideas are. So he said as far as he was concerned, you were no longer my husband. I should forget you. Joan, if she ever asks about her father, will be told you have died somewhere far away.

So that's how it is. I thought at least you would like to know the situation.

I have to admit, I'm disappointed with you, James. Maybe one day you'll be a better man. God forgive and support you.

    Eliza"

For the first time for years James stopped short. As much as he tried to pretend that he wasn't hurt by Eliza's words, the news of his poor old dad did make him realise just how much he had let his father down. The old man deserved better of his family and James was sorry he had missed his funeral. As for Eliza, well, she never really loved him anyway. And as for Eliza's father's phrase, "you were not fit to live," – well, who was he to judge?

So he shrugged that whole period of his life aside. Susanna insisted on reading the letter. Her response was, "You weren't fair with that woman. I know what you're up to. All I ask is that you keep your kids out of your business and pay me regularly for rent and their upkeep. I can live with the rest for now. Just don't step out of line with me."

James would settle with that. There was no point in sitting there moping about the past. He had his own family now with Susanna and Harry. He had done alright in the end. "You have to make your own luck in life," he said to himself. As crime continued to pay, so his family continued to get bigger. Within five years, there was John, William James and Emily, though she died soon after her second birthday from scarlet fever.

*

William James had always been called Will for as long as he could remember. His dad didn't seem to be around much so Harry behaved like he was the man of the house. Already by the age of twelve Harry was tall and strong and had started working in the building trade.

Will felt very close to his mother. She was the one who taught them all how to read. Counting, she thought, you picked up by yourself. There was no formal schooling for any of them. Somehow dad provided enough money for them to have at least shoes to wear.

John and Will used to play in the open fields around the estate. But it wasn't long before they began to notice lots more houses being built. As soon as the houses were finished, large numbers of people moved onto the estate. The brothers soon met other children from these families but found it difficult to understand what they were saying.

When they told their mum, she said, "They've come from Ireland."

"Why have they come here?" asked John.

"We hear they came over to England to escape what I've been told was a great famine. Not sure what I make of the Irish. People say you should be careful. You never know whether they carry illnesses and diseases. Stick to your own kind, I say."

Even at that age, Will found it hard to believe that you could die just by mixing with strange people. He obeyed his mum and as a result he never got to know any of the Irish kids on the estate.

Dad was a mysterious figure in their lives. When he was at home, he could be great fun. He also liked to take the whole family out on trips into Essex. Dad regarded these trips to Epping Forest as a chance to be one big jolly family. From nowhere he would turn up one day with a horse and cart, big enough for all of them to pile into. Mother would put together some bread, cheese, apples and milk for a picnic in the forest.

It was on one of these trips, when Will was eight years old, that he found out more about what his dad got up to. Will was at the age when he was curious enough to want to ask questions about everything.

"Are we going to the same place as last time, dad?" he asked, "What's it called?"

"Yes, son, we're going to Lambourne so you can have fun in Hainault forest."

"Dad, why is it that, when we get there, you go off somewhere on your own?" was Will's next question.

"Coz I have to," replied dad sharply.

Will looked across at his mother's face. There was a frown on her face. Will was worried he had said the wrong thing. He decided to keep quiet for now.

It wasn't long before Will recognised that they were getting near the forest. He felt a wish not to be separated from his dad. His dad was always going off and leaving them. So Will plucked up the courage to ask, "Can I come with you, Dad, just for once?"

"No, son, that wouldn't be possible," he replied.

Before Will could ask the inevitable, "Why not?" Will's mother stepped in.

"I think at least you could take Will and the boys to see their grandma and grandpa's grave."

Dad stopped the cart. He was clearly angry. But mother kept her nerve.

"They need to see a bit more of the place you and your family lived in. It would do them good."

"Alright," said dad, "but we'll have to be a bit sharpish about it. I've got some business to do this afternoon."

"I know all about that, but you take them anyway. It won't hurt you for once."

Dad gave in. It was only a short journey they made and dad knew where he was going well enough. They arrived at a church. Will's dad tied up the horse and led his family to a particular grave. There they saw a headstone dedicated to the memory of Betsy Walton, her ten day-old daughter Sarah and Henry Walton, the father.

Will read these words and out came more questions. "1852, that's not long ago. You never told us your dad died then. And why did Sarah die?"

"Hard to explain, son," replied his dad, "except to say that no baby can survive without its mother to feed it. Now let's be going. You've seen where my mum and dad are buried." He started to move away.

"But, Dad, you never talk about your mum and dad. What were they like? Were you sad when they died?"

"Stop asking Dad questions, Will," chipped in his brother Harry.

"It's alright Harry," said his dad. "All I would say about my mum and dad is that they were both good people who had a hard life."

"Why don't you tell us more about them?" Will was ignorant of the fact that he was winding up his father terribly.

"That's enough, Will. Why are you always asking questions? They've been and gone, and that's it. Now come on."

Mother rose to Will's defence. "The lad only wants to know about his grandparents, no harm in that. Don't scold him just for being interested."

Will's dad did not reply. Will meanwhile looked at his mother. He sensed at that early age that he had her support when it came to trying to understand his dad better.

They all got into the cart. Will's mother then said, "Your old home isn't far away, is it?"

They all sensed their dad's uncomfortable feelings about what was happening. He felt he was losing control of the situation, as well as his temper. The past was clearly something he did not want to talk about. Still, he had to pretend to hang onto the belief that the day was meant to be a family day out.

"Somewhere over the brow of that hill ahead I reckon. It was only a courtyard, one room – no more than that – where we stayed."

"Is it still there?" asked Will.

"Perhaps, I don't know," said his dad, "Now, that's enough. I want us to get to a nice spot to sit down and have some food. You must all be hungry by now."

"I'm starving," said John.

"You can't say you're starving because actually you've never known what starving is like," said dad. He was still very irritable.

Will was about to ask another question when his mother stepped in and said, "Now, be quiet Will." Will closed his mouth.

The family settled down to eat their food. Dad, after just a few bites, got up and said he would be back soon. Off he went in the cart. Nobody said anything.

Dad returned an hour or so later. In the cart were a sack and a basket full of eggs. "A good haul, I'd say. Eggs and a couple of rabbits." None of the children asked where they had come from, assuming as children do, that they had been bought.

"Your friends look after you, don't they?" said Mum.

"Share and share alike, I say," replied Dad.

His mood was considerably improved. The children felt it was safe to ask questions.

"Did your family all come from this part of Essex?" asked Harry.

"Naw," replied Dad, "We originally came from Rayleigh."

"Why did you move to Abridge?" asked Harry.

"We were turfed off the land by the landowner and had to find somewhere else to live."

"What did your dad do for a living?" asked Harry.

"He worked as a coach builder," said dad.

"Why don't you do the same?" asked Will.

"'Cos I couldn't take to it," replied dad, with a little irritation in his voice.

Will's brother John decided it was alright for him to ask a question for a change. "If you liked it so much round here, in Essex, how come you left Essex and came to live where we are now?"

Their dad went very quiet. After a few moments he simply said, "Let's just say I had to."

Will could not hold back his question. "Dad, did you have any brothers and sisters?

"I had a brother but I think he now lives in Canada," replied dad.

"Why did he go there?"

"Cos he chose to. Now, that's enough. No more questions, you lot. Let's enjoy the ride home."

Will cast a glance at his mother. She turned to her son and with a quick movement of her head skywards, gave him the impression that all was not what it seemed in what Dad was saying. These unresolved questions Will was determined to get to the bottom of one day when he was older. Like any young boy he wanted to get to know his father better, if he could.

CHAPTER 5

Love and Loathing

"Wirr be gwain to, Will?"

William James Walton, now a tall young man with dark hair and brown eyes, was about to leave the house where he lived, when he heard a familiar voice. Turning round, Will saw the head of Mary emerging from behind the scullery door.

"Tiz getting dimpsey," Mary said.

"Getting 'dimpsey', what's that word mean? You don't half talk funny, Mary Badman."

Mary quickly turned and heard the mischievous tone in Will's voice. She retaliated by putting on her heaviest accent.

"Don't ye forget. A be vrom Zummerzet. Tis' the speech of King Arthur's court, so a be told. A's talk proper English." This last word was said in a posh voice, imitating the speech of a high-class lady.

"Don't sound proper nuffinck." Will replied with an exaggerated Cockney accent. "Just plain 'daffadown dilly' – that means silly to you, by the way."

"Hark at he," chipped in Mary's brother, Joseph. "We don't reckon your cockney accent makes much sense either." He was sitting on the porch steps, smoking his pipe.

"Well, that's true, I suppose, but I'm not a true cockney. You have to have been born within the sound of Bow Bells to call yourself that," Will replied. After a short pause he said, "By the way, Mary, what does 'dimpsey' mean?"

"End of day, twilight, you 'doughboy' – that means dumpling by the way," Mary said.

"Alright, Mary, I give in," Will said. "Now just let me get past the gate and I'll be back soon. I'm going up the road to see my folks. I haven't seen them for some time now. Mum and my younger brother and sister will be there. I just hope my dad's out."

"Well you do make it obvious that you don't get on with your dad," said Mary.

"Would you be proud of a dad who's a rogue and a thief? Who doesn't worry who he hurts as long as he's OK. Someone who makes money out of the hardship of others. Well, anyway, mum's owed a visit. I shan't be long. No trips to the rubba-dub-dub – that's pub to you. Will you be here, the pair of you?"

"To be sure," said Joe. "We're not likely to be done and be let off by the mistress of the house for a while yet."

Mary gave Will one of her gorgeous smiles, her blue eyes twinkling in that soft round face of hers. "Behave yourself, Will, and don't be long."

As he set off down the road, Will's head was buzzing at the thought of the night of their first kiss. The excitement of that moment – what a girl! What a lucky thing it was that they had all met at the house. Back in Somerset, Mary had persuaded her brother Joseph to go with her to London. At the same time a local dressmaker, Elizabeth Butler, decided she would like to come as well. All three of them were hopeful that things had to be better than back in Somerset. They had stuck together and had been lucky enough to get work together at Albion House. That's where they met up with Will. For his first job he had been fortunate enough to get a job near his home and with employers who had required him to live on their premises. That eased the crowding in his tiny house in Bride Street.

Will had been taken on as a handyman. Joseph was the gardener, Mary the chambermaid and Elizabeth worked in the parlour. Mary and Elizabeth shared a room at the top of the house, opposite the room which Will shared with Joseph. After a few months Elizabeth was able to find work in a clothes factory in Whitechapel.

The owners of the house and its grounds were Mr and Mrs Littlejohn. They were kind enough in their own way but they expected their servants to be docile and obedient whilst meeting all their employers' constant demands, night and day. In this respect the daughters of the house were worst of all – Will liked to think they were a bit jealous of his Mary's looks, but then he knew he might be biased. The Littlejohns' son was alright but always out working in Clerkenwell, in a bank perhaps.

The four of them – Will, Mary, Joseph and Elizabeth – would enjoy a once-a-month visit to the Caledonian Arms for a drink and a sing-song. Mary enjoyed people and made them laugh. She had a lovely voice and was often asked to sing songs she knew from the West Country.

Joseph quickly noticed his sister and Will getting on so well, but he didn't see any need to protect her. "She can look after herself," he said when Mary and Will mentioned going for a walk around the open spaces of Holloway and towards Highgate. "I don't see as how there's any need for me to accompany you two."

She was the same age as Will – twenty years old but much more forward. On the walk she gripped Will's arm while she talked about her home in a tiny hamlet called Calcott.

"What was life like back there in the village? It sounds all very peaceful and quiet," said Will.

"That's per'aps true but there were few choices for girls," replied Mary. "In the country you either had to go into domestic service or you became a farmer's wife. Not much changes. Even if you happened to have got some education, you might become a governess, but that wasn't much better. So I made up my mind to leave and come to London in the hope of finding more opportunities for work."

"So what do you think of London then?" Will asked.

"Well, it's so huge compared with my village and people move so fast. But London is exciting and different. Not that I've seen too much so far."

Will interrupted her. "London also has masses of poor people, half of them starving. There's lots of crime. And meanwhile the rich have so much money which they constantly wave in your face."

"Now, Will, that's enough of that," Mary said firmly. "While I'm walking out with you, I want you to relax and for us to enjoy each other's company. Don't forget it's London that made it possible for us to meet. We get so little time off, let's enjoy our time together."

Will took the hint. As they came back along a footpath near the Caledonian Arms, they had shared their first kiss. Both were very nervous and excited and did not know what to do next. Will suggested they go for a drink. After that, they walked back home, very happy. She was giggling while Will was shaking his head in disbelief at what was happening between them. The next Sunday they were both free for a couple of hours, so Will had taken Mary to meet his mum. Mary got on well with Charlie and Alice, the youngest members of the family.

By now Will had walked past Mountford House, the poshest building in the district. Round this little area, the street was cobbled as opposed to the usual mud tracks. Soon after he reached Henry Place in Bride Street, he had already been spotted by Charlie. Will heard him shout, "It's Will, Mum." Will's young sister, Alice, then came rushing out the door to greet him. Will stepped over the front door step and went along a short corridor till he reached the kitchen.

Soon he was sitting down with his mother, drinking a mug of tea. "Is Harry still working around Hoxton?" Will asked.

"Yes," said his mum, "some construction job. John is managing to earn a few pennies doing some gardening work out Hornsey way. There's not much work here in Barnsbury."

It was a familiar routine. Mum was reciting what each of her children was up to. It was now Will's turn to be questioned.

"And how's work at Albion House? Is it secure?"

"It's alright, Mum," Will replied. "Sometimes it gets very busy, working all hours freeing the drains, fixing fences or repairing bits of furniture. Still I've become quite useful as a handyman and it's a job for now."

Then the inevitable question. "And how's that lovely girl you brought here?" By now all her attention was fixed on every word that he said.

"She's doing alright, settling down well in London. By the way, she did enjoy meeting you all the other week. You cheered her up and made her less homesick."

Will was ready and prepared for the next question.

"And are you going together seriously?" came mother's innocent question.

"I don't know, Mum. I like her but I wouldn't want to tie her down. She may want to move on to a better position. She's been at the house six months. I'd be sorry if she went, but I don't know."

"Don't know what, William? You like her and it's obvious she likes you."

"Well, I don't know whether it will be me who moves away, even as far as Canada where my uncle went. I also feel I want to get myself more education. I want to understand what's going on around me. Like, there's so much going on with new industries and jobs down the docks in east London.

"I also want to get involved with other men fighting to get something better for themselves and their families, standing up and fighting for what's right – better wages and working conditions, better housing. Things like that I think are important. I'm not sure I can settle down with all this buzzing round my head."

Mum shook her head. "My God, you're different to your dad. He'd say you're crazy. Will, I appreciate some of what you're saying. A man has got to work out how he can improve himself. And I know you always wanted to get some more learning. I wouldn't want to stop you. I only ask you not to overdo it. Have you thought whether Mary might be just the person to help you? A good woman will always be the best friend you'll ever have. After your mum, that is. Mary's a good woman with a good heart and plenty of sense. Take your chance, don't hesitate."

Will tried to change tack. "You know if she wants to work, we can't get married," said Will.

"Yes, I know it's tough on women – they're told to either get a fella or get a job," mum added, "so she'll have

57

to pretend she doesn't know you. Besides, there's plenty of couples not married. Most of us don't see the point. Your dad and I aren't married. Mind you, your dad's been married before – ask him about it sometime when you see him."

"Well, I never knew that."

To change the subject, Will asked innocently, "Is dad around then?"

"Are you kidding? He's not been here for days. He came home last week, threw his arms around me and made me a gift of some silver earrings. 'Where'd you get these,' I asked. 'I bought them for you,' he said. My Lord, how his breath smelt of booze. Well, you know your father. He would not say any more about anything. He tried to insist on me trying them on. 'What, while I'm working in the kitchen? Don't be daft,' I said. He put the earrings down on the table and turned to face the boys. But after a couple of minutes, he left."

"So, I wonder what he's up to now?" Will said. "I'm going to find out sometime, sooner or later."

"Well, don't ask me," said mum. "Still, at least before he left he gave me a few quid for food and paying the bills. Said he'd see me on Thursday."

"That's a couple of days time. Mum, do me a favour. When he does come and if he's stopping the night, let me know, will you? Just send Charlie up the road to where I work – it's only half a mile away."

His mum had agreed and that's how it happened. Two days later Charlie came to the side entrance of

Albion House to tell Will his dad was at home that evening. That same evening Will went and asked his employer, Mr Littlejohn, if he could be absent on the Friday morning in order to attend to some family business. Mr Littlejohn, without consulting his wife, (who would probably have said no), agreed.

Next morning Will got up early and walked quickly round to Bride Street. Instead of going in, he hid outside within sight of the house. He was relying on the fact that his dad rarely got up early after a night's drinking. Then, suddenly, there he was.

You could tell James Walton was no working man – he was always trying to look smart with a proper jacket and pressed trousers, with hat and tie. But he was kidding himself – the outfit was crumpled and beer-stained and his shoes were pretty worn. In winter he wore an old scarf which had seen better days.

He set off at a fair pace, walking down towards the City. Will kept up with him, at a distance.

The Whitechapel Road presented an amazing sight. It was one of the twice-weekly market days when farmers came from all over Essex. Cartloads of hay were lined up in the road, waiting to be unloaded. In the middle of the road herds of cows, sheep and horses roamed. Most of them were going to be sold and sent to the slaughterhouses in Whitechapel. The horses were also traded, as was the hay.

Accompanying the scene were what seemed like hundreds of women standing around, especially near the pubs. With their hair-dos, fancy hats made from colourful bird feathers, revealing dresses and red coloured lips, trade was also brisk for the prostitutes of the area.

James Walton made for one large pub and crept in by a side entrance, looking round in all directions before closing the door. Less than half an hour later, he came out with a box, carefully packed with a string handle. The box was clearly a bit heavy. Will's dad then made his way to a bus stop and took a bus going up Kingsland Road towards Stoke Newington. Will got on the same bus, keeping well away from where his dad was sitting, hiding his face.

His dad got up to get off at Balls Pond Road. With Will still tailing him, he walked a short distance to a small warehouse and went inside. From the hammering noise inside and the flick of flames glowing above a door, it seemed to be some kind of smelting works. A few minutes later, he came out without the box. As he walked away, Will decided this was the time to confront him. He stepped out from a side entrance and stood in front of him.

"What were you carrying in that box, Dad?" Will asked.

For a second his dad was startled but he quickly recovered himself. "Oh, hello Will, fancy seeing you here. Is your mother alright or why else have you come right up here? Can't be just to see me."

"Dad, you didn't answer my question."

"So, your mother's alright then – that's good news. Well, son, what do you want to know?"

"Did it contain silver-ware?" Will asked.

"Look, as far as I'm concerned the box contained bits and pieces I was carrying for a friend, to deliver them on his behalf, acting like a supplier if you like."

"Were they stolen goods?"

"How should I know? I only fetch and carry, the rest is other people's business."

Will wanted to raise the stakes in their conversation. "I hear talk of stolen goods, especially silver, being passed around the North London area – from an off-duty copper I met in a pub."

"Stone the crows! My son a friend of a copper! That's a right turn up! But I suppose coppers are just like any other bloke trying to make a living somehow."

"Do you make yours by thieving or being an accessory, as they say?"

"Son, don't make me angry by making accusations when you don't know if they're true or not. What's my business is my business. Haven't I looked after my family all these years and helped them get jobs where I can? Look, son, I know I'm not the best of fathers, being absent and all that.. yes and the booze…

"Blimey, why am I talking to you like this? Must be something in those eyes of yours. Maybe you understand me too well. Look, Will, what I'm trying to say is that I do care about your mum and my family. If anything happens to me, there'll be some money about to look after them. I am what I am and that's that."

"What's that, Dad?" Will interrupted. "I want to hear it from you."

"Well, I suppose I'm a bit of a rogue, really. Look, son, if the rich had their choice they wouldn't give you nothing. So the poor man can do himself a favour by helping himself where he can…helping to redistribute goods if you like to call it that… without the law's permission you might say.

"I don't do anything criminal by my book. I'm only the middleman, mind you. I don't really get involved with thievery – I just move things around from one owner to another and get paid a bit for my trouble. Is that so bad?"

"I know, you're called a fence. But you're not earning your money by honest labour. Is it fair on those whose stuff you nick?" Will was becoming insistent.

"Don't give me all that talk about honesty and fairness. Believe it or not, I've got a brother John. He believed in standing up and being counted in the fight with the bosses. And what good did that do him? It got him time in the nick on trumped-up charges. He hopped it to Canada to make a fresh start. Some'ow I don't fancy Canada. I prefer to make my way in London, doing what I'm good at. That makes me an honest man to my way of thinking.

"And what about you? You've got a handyman job up the road – good for you I say – but how far is that going to get you when their lordships decide to get rid of you because you've somehow offended them for no reason at all, though probably your tongue will get you into trouble for speaking your mind. What's fair about that?

"Where's your security and how are you going to look after that lovely girl your mother told me about? A man needs money and if he's poor, he's got a right to get it anyway he can – as long as nobody gets hurt, mind you, no violence."

"Have you ever been had up for breaking the law or have you just been lucky enough not to get caught?" Will kept his questions coming.

"I haven't been caught. That's because I mind my back and always give people sweeteners to keep them happy," Dad replied.

"Dad, I can't be like you. There's a big struggle going to take place when working men stand up and demand a fairer share in work, money and health for themselves and their families. I want to be part of that fight and be proud to stand shoulder to shoulder with other workers, not slink off down dodgy streets carrying stolen loot and sniffing the air like a rat in the sewers."

"You're saying some harsh things about me, son, but I can't get upset too much with you. Somehow I might even like you for speaking your mind. Now, come on, let's change the subject. Do me a favour and go home. Tell your mother I'll be back in a day or so. Here – give her a few bob from me for the rent – six and six pence a week, isn't it?"

Will showed great reluctance to take it, so his dad was the one who became persistent.

"Go on, son. Take it for your mother's sake, if not for mine. You're old enough now to understand why I need you to keep me a little bit straight and be mindful of my duties to you all. Please take it."

The coins were thrust into Will's hands. He closed his fist over them.

"Alright, Dad, for mum's sake. Though I still think you could give it to her yourself and not use me as a go-between."

"Well, Will, your older brothers have helped me in a similar way in the past and they've moved away. Where you live now, you can keep an eye out for your mother for me. Only till I'm back, mind you. Right, that's it. I must go and so must you. See you son."

And with that, he swiftly moved off. He disappeared down a side street – no doubt to some pub Will thought.

Will stood there, confused and angry. "How does my dad always get away with it – conning people – my mum, my brothers and now me – in accepting what he does? He gets round us all with his words. He is the original artful dodger."

CHAPTER 6

Tidal Basin

"I've been a thinking we could try our luck in West Ham," suggested Joe one evening down at the 'Cale Arms'. "Since the opening of Royal Victoria Dock, big iron ships have been able to get further up the river and all sorts of new firms have been moving there and that must mean lots of jobs."

"As I heard it, they've got some heavy industries set up now," joined in Will. "There's Thames Ironworks making ships, chemical works, sugar refiners, flour-milling and loads more. When you think about what's coming in – coal, sugar, wheat, rubber, tobacco – from all over the Empire – well, that means lots of warehouses and factories, railways to take the stuff away and, as you say Joe, plenty of jobs."

"So what are you suggesting Joe?" said Mary, "That you want to give up your job here and move to dockland? Would there be anywhere to live down there? Or are you thinking of just getting up and going and hoping for the best?"

"I'm sure there would be," said Will. "Employers generally like their workers staying near their premises. That's been the pattern from other places like the North of England, so I'm told."

"Don't the factories come first and the homes later?" asked Mary. "Are you going to check first? By the way, who's involved in this plan?"

"I'm in for taking our chances," said Joe. "After all, Mary, we gave up everything in Somerset to come to London. It's worked well for us so far."

"That's no guarantee for the future and you know it, brother," said Mary. "What about you Will? I take it you'd be prepared to move if Joe did."

"Yes, I'll give it a go. I'm fed up with the work here. There'll be more going on in the East End than here in Islington. And I for one was kind of hoping, you'd come too, Mary."

"Well, I sort of like the idea of a change. And I do believe we should stick together. I shall make my own enquiries about places to stay. The cook at the Littlejohns place, she said she came from nearby Canning Town and was glad to get away from the place as being too rough for her. I'll see what she says."

"I'd be sorry to leave you behind," said Will and he squeezed Mary's hand.

Some months later Will, Mary and Joe, set off for West Ham. What a shock they had as they walked across the River Lea at Bow Bridge and saw a huge cement manufacturing plant. "That's for all those new houses we'll find," said Joe. They turned south, in the direction of the Thames, until they reached this long road called Victoria Dock Road.

From where they stood, they could see the shape of the cranes and the ship yards of Thames Ironworks and some of the ships in Victoria Dock. These shapes dwarfed the houses and stuck out like menacing monsters, emerging from the gloom of the heavy mist and dirty smoke which were pouring out of the many chimney stacks.

"The sun will have a hard job penetrating through this lot," remarked Joe.

"And I don't see how anyone can keep anything clean for long round here," added Mary.

It was decided it might be best to go into one of the many pubs to enquire after accommodation. They walked into the Red Lion, and began asking around if there was anywhere with a room or two to let. They were lucky. A man called Tom said, "Me and two other dockers are sharing a house in Charlotte Street. We've got the two upper rooms. We're looking for people to take the two rooms below. Are you interested?"

"What's the rent?" asked Joe.

"Six bob a week."

"That seems fair enough. We'll take them."

Islington had seemed built-up enough but what they were looking at now comprised street after street of back-to-back houses, closely packed together with narrow passageways at the rear. One building stood out though.

It was a big church called St. Luke's. Turning a corner, they soon found Charlotte Street.

No 42, like all the houses in Charlotte Street, wasn't very old but already it looked shabby. Everywhere felt damp and cold.

The first thing Mary wanted to check was the water supply. "Washing and cleaning are pretty important I'd say – and then how to keep warm." In a small room at the rear there was a range fire and a copper. In the backyard Mary saw there was a mangle, scrubbing board and a tub for baths. Nearby was a standing tap for water.

Next to the yard fence was the privy. Will noticed that it was little more than a hole in the ground. Waste would just go out into a covered ditch along the back passage between the houses. Since the terrible outbreak of 1866, everybody knew that cholera was the name of the illness which had caused many deaths in the East End; also that its spread was linked to the lack of drainage for waste water.

Someone looked over the next-door fence. "Hello, you just moving in?" asked a voice.

"Yes," said Mary. "I'm Mary, this is Joe and this is Will."

"I'm Jane," replied the neighbour. "What do you think of the place? Pretty lousy isn't it? They're all the same – cheap to build and put in the wrong place."

"What do you mean wrong place?" Will asked.

"You wait and see when the next high tide or heavy rain comes. All these houses in this area are below the level of the River Thames. So when it overflows, particularly in winter, you can get water down the street and into the houses. It floods the ditches as well. That means the tap water is no good. All the water comes from the Thames anyway."

"Thanks for telling us," said Mary, "though I'm not sure I wanted to know that."

"Has this area got a name?" asked Will.

"Tidal Basin."

"Makes sense, given what you've just told us about flooded streets," remarked Joe.

They all smiled at each other. "I'd better leave you to get sorted out," said Jane. "Bye for now." Her head disappeared back over the fence.

There was hardly any furniture. The bedding consisted of old mattresses on the floor. This was not a good idea as fleas and bedbugs could easily make a home in them. Mary suspected there could also be the occasional rat. But at least they had new paraffin lamps, instead of candles. And it was a place to stay.

The next task was for Will and Joe to find jobs. They wandered around together, past the shipyards, the warehouses and the factories. "Don't fancy being a docker myself," said Joe. "Looks pretty dangerous to me, all those cranes with heavy loads flying about over your head."

"OK, let's try one of the warehouses," said Will. Just then a coal wagon passed. Joe looked at the horses pulling the cart and exclaimed, "That's it. Let's try a coal warehouse. I can say I've worked with horses before back in Somerset."

So they entered a coal yard, found the foreman and asked if there were two jobs going. The first question the foreman asked was, "Ever worked with horses before?" Joe was right – he got them the job. "You'll start work tomorrow. Be here at 6 o'clock. If you're lucky you'll get off around 8 pm. Ever lifted one hundredweight sacks before? They're heavy enough, especially if you have to walk far with one over your head. You'll be expected to deliver about sixty to eighty sacks every day. You've probably seen one of the leather hoods we use to protect our ears and head. It's got a studded leather guard, which you position over your shoulder to prevent the coal from digging into yer back. Any questions? No? Now if you complete your quota, between you you'll get eight shillings a day. You'll also be paid an extra shilling for driving the horse and one penny for watering him. Alright then, I'll see you tomorrow."

Joe and Will walked away. "That's not bad money. Much better than the miserable couple of quid we earned at the Littlejohns," said Will.

Next day, they got started. The cart was already loaded, the horse just needed saddling up. They were now officially called carmen. They were given their list of places to deliver their load. Sometimes it was a household but often it was business premises. They soon got into the swing of things. The biggest challenge was

70

the moment when the weight of each sack transferred from the cart to their backs, with one hand holding the top of the sack while the other kept the load stable.

However whether or not they delivered all they were expected to deliver each day was largely beyond their control. Delays could usually be expected whenever they had to cross the swing bridge at Tidal Basin. Whenever it was high tide large vessels would be passing in or out of Victoria Docks into or from the Thames. Up went the swing bridge. All the traffic, and there was often lots of it, had to wait. When the bridge came down, the traffic moved in single file to the other side. 'Catching a bridger,' it was called. Then there were the delays caused by being held up at the railway level crossing for the frequent trains taking goods away from the docks. Joe was much more patient than Will about the delays, although both new it would cost them money.

One thing both Joe and Will liked about the job was meeting lots of different people. One day, not long after starting work as carmen, Will and Joe had an unusual order to deliver domestic coal to the offices of Thames Ironworks. Visiting Thames Ironworks had been quite an experience because it was so huge. There were slipways where ships were being constructed and lots of railway tracks criss-crossing the area.

Small steam trains with their wagons used these tracks to supply materials to wherever they were needed on site. To reach the area where Will and Joe were to deliver the coal, they had to drive around the tracks whilst avoiding the trains which constantly moved back and forth.

The driver of one of these trains hooted as they approached the line he was using. They stopped the horse. "Ta, mate," said the driver and waved.

Will looked at the driver's face and immediately said, "Here, don't I know you?"

The driver brought his train to a halt. "Maybe," said the driver, "everybody gets to know everybody round here."

"My mate and I moved into Charlotte Street a few weeks back, number 42," said Will. "I thought I saw you next door – could we be neighbours?"

"Naw, you're getting me mixed up with my brother Frederick who lives at number 44," replied the driver. "I look a lot like him. No, I live round the corner in Hack Road. We both work here but his job is to maintain the trains. What's your name, mate?"

"Will. Will Walton and this is Joe Badman." Joe nodded.

"Pleased to meet you both. My name is Walter Horth."

After a short pause, Walter, with a smile on his face said, "I'll tell you what. I'd rather have my job than yours – all that humping coal and getting covered in soot."

"Ah, it's alright," Joe said, "money's not too bad."

"What time you likely to finish today?" asked Walter.

"Around 8pm, if we're lucky," replied Joe.

"You know the Hallsville Tavern, in Hallsville Road?"

asked Walter. Joe nodded. "Well, if you fancy a pint after work, I'll see you in there, right?"

That evening, after dropping their horse and cart off at the depot, they set off for the Hallsville, a pub they hadn't used before, which was not surprising since there were so many in Tidal Basin. They went into the public bar and soon spotted Walter. The place may have been crowded but Walter was conspicuous by his loud laughter. He was with another man. The family resemblance was obvious. They were also both big fellows. Will was just under six foot but these two towered over him. They approached Walter.

"Wotcha. Will and Joe isn't it," said Walter. "This here's my brother Frederick. A word of warning – he likes to be called that and not Fred. He's not as handsome as me, but probably he's got more grey matter in his head."

Frederick smiled and they all shook hands.

"What would you like to drink?" asked Walter. Joe went for a pint of mild and bitter and Will for straight bitter. Walter swiftly got the barmaid's attention and they quickly got served.

"So, how long have you been in the area?" asked Frederick.

"Not long," said Joe, "we've come down here from Islington, though I originally come from Somerset. Will's from Islington though."

"S'ppose you came looking for work," said Walter. "That's why most people come here. So, what d'yer think of the houses, eh? Awful, ain't they? Thrown up in a hurry they were – with no by your leave from anybody – no planning permission and that sort of thing, not nuffing. I know for a fact that the local board aren't happy about things, especially the lack of proper sewers."

"That's why a lot of people are asking for West Ham to become a borough with powers to force the owners and landlords to make changes," said Frederick. "But, to change the subject, did you bring any family with you?"

"Just me," replied Will.

"And I'm here with my sister," said Joe. "What about yourselves?"

"Oh, us! The Horths are everywhere round here," said Walter. "There's our own three brothers and two sisters and their families scattered all round Tidal Basin. You can hardly avoid running into a Horth somewhere or other in the area."

"Are your mum and dad still alive?" asked Joe.

Frederick replied, "Unfortunately, both our parents died recently. They came from Essex many years ago – among the first wave, if you like, into the area. And your parents?"

Joe and Will announced both their parents were still living.

Walter, who obviously liked talking, stepped in. "One peculiar thing about the names of all my brothers, is that we all have the name Watling. Now I know it's normal to name your kids with the same names as yourself or the grandparents – I mean all our boys have names like George, Charles, Henry, Thomas and the girls names like Emma but this Watling bit also goes back generations with each son being expected to carry it. I think after my third son, I gave up the idea. Couldn't make sense of it."

"Sounds like somebody trying to be posh," Joe suggested.

"Nobody's posh in Tidal Basin," replied Walter.

"So, what do you two do when you're not working?" asked Frederick.

"I try to get the chance to read the newspapers, if I can," replied Will." I like to find out what's going on – and to improve my knowledge."

"You want to become a scholar or something. I can't see the point," chipped in Walter, in a jokey voice.

"Walter, that's because you're not bothered," said his brother. "Listen, Will, would you like to get into the Mechanics Institute in Stratford? They have a library and reading room. If you like I can see about getting a membership form. I'll propose you and someone else will second you. Are you interested?"

Will was unable to hold back his excitement. "You bet," he said.

"What about you, Joe?" asked Frederick.

"Sure I'll come along and see what it's like. Would I be right in thinking they'll have games like draughts or quoits there as well?" asked Joe. "That would be right kind of you. Thanks."

Will would always be grateful to Frederick Horth. He was as good as his word. With Frederick's help Will was able to get into the Mechanics Institute. Frederick also obtained a membership card at the Working Men's Club in Victoria Dock for Joe and himself.

Will's life had changed enormously from that moment. Most days became the same – long hours of delivering coal, then down to the Institute to get into the library when it was open. Once inside the door, he headed for the newspapers. Will had always been fascinated by the idea of reading about what was going on in the streets and areas where he lived, as well as what was happening elsewhere. Now he had the chance to find out for himself.

Armed with a dictionary for words and places he had never heard about, he devoured the news. He also found out what exactly the British Empire consisted of and now he could find out about the countries where these raw materials he had seen came from. No more was he reliant on rumour and the implausible stories that were supposed to have taken place. Now he could read the facts.

Frederick and Will got on well together. What they shared, apart from a pint of beer, was a love of reading and talking. When they met up in the evenings, both would look forward to a good conversation because they recognised each other as being as different as chalk and cheese, with very different opinions.

"Will, you're an impatient man. I watch you getting angry whenever you hear about someone cheating, or somebody trying to lord it over others. Your eyes light up and your breathing becomes heavier."

"And you, Frederick, never get angry. You are a placid, tolerant, kindly man. You never want to offend anybody and would go out of your way to help others," Will replied.

A short pause, then one would open up on a topic to discuss.

"When did you first start to get curious about books and learning?" asked Will.

"Probably, like everything else to do with the Horths, it started with religion," said Frederick. "Our parents were always reading the Bible or books like 'Pilgrim's Progress' to us. As we got older and attended Sunday School, father began to invite us to read the Bible out loud. If we didn't understand a word, Dad would say, 'look it up in the dictionary, will you'. That's how I came to love books. What about you, Will?"

"I suppose you would call me self-taught," replied Will. "I never went to any Sunday school or anything like that. Luckily my mum was able to teach us the basics of reading and counting. The rest I picked up for myself. This place has been fantastic for me. This library's like my church, I can get all I need here," said Will.

"If you've never been to a church much in your life, you perhaps don't know what you're missing."

"I'm not sure about religion and faith. It's never featured in my family's upbringing, whereas in yours it did."

"I have followed the ways of my parents and grandparents," continued Frederick, "because it offered me a guide and a rock upon which to build my life. It continues to be the way I view the world and I try to live my life as a follower of the teachings of Jesus Christ."

"I don't see the point in church services and ceremonies," said Will. "Who are we trying to reach to out there? And God, if he did exist, would he be interested in us as individuals? Do we need an outsider to help run our lives?"

"But you're only thinking of yourself. You're missing the satisfaction of people coming together to show their joy in being alive and in trying to help the less fortunate. Faith also gives you the confident belief that when this life is over, we shall have a resting place in Heaven. That's why Jane and I are Christians – it is a source of inspiration to help others."

"I can see that having faith can be comforting when times get rough," replied Will. "It is perhaps humbling to realise that something is bigger than yourself. Recently I read about a chaplain whose congregation was the light-house keepers and the seamen whom the chaplain visited whenever a boat came across with fresh provisions. One of the crew members had told him, 'You won't find many Christians around us lot, but when the storms rage fiercely, there're not many atheists either.'

"In some ways I could envy you, Frederick, but then it's all a matter of what you want to believe."

"If something terrible happens, you may find yourself in need of God's love."

"By the way, changing the subject, I didn't realise that Jane and you are expecting your first child."

"Yes, hopefully. If it's a boy, he'll be called Frederick while if it's a girl, she will be named Emma. He or she will be baptised in the name of Christ so that, should they die young, they will receive his promise of eternal life."

CHAPTER 7

Relationship under Strain

"I'm going to be very careful not to get pregnant or they'll make me leave any job I've got. So I'm afraid you'll have to come to terms with keeping it tucked away, as they say, as well as us not getting married." Mary decided now was the time to make her position clear.

Joe was out again. He had given up the Mechanics Institute for the dance floor. He left Will and Mary alone to carry on as they wished. By now Mary had fixed ideas as to what she wanted from their relationship.

"A lot of women, when they're hardly grown up, get pregnant too easily. They end up being expected to go on producing kids year after year, as well as looking after a house. They often have to deal with husbands who drink too much because they don't always manage to be in work. The men get frustrated and often take their anger and frustration out on their missus and their kids. It's the women who suffer when rents don't get paid and kids go hungry.

"It doesn't have to be like that," said Will.

"Believe you me, Will, I've seen it happen in my own family and I am determined not to go the same way. Just look at many of the women round here – worn out, looking old before their time and unhappy. They're tough of course – women have to be – but it's no life. Only constant drudgery and hardship. And prostitution is no real choice either. I know there are hundreds of them earning cash off the thousands of seamen who pass though Tidal Basin, but it's dangerous and likely to get them the clap."

"So what else is there – for women, I mean?" asked Will.

"You men don't get it, do you? Look, why should half of the population not have the chance to show they can do more than factory work or domestic service or be pressured into getting married?"

"What do you want to do for yourself then?" asked a confused Will.

"I'm not sure yet but I think I want to become a nurse, if I can," Mary replied.

"That will require lots of training, won't it?" said Will. "Aren't you being a bit ambitious? And won't it require us splitting up? You'll have to live where you work, won't you?"

"Oh Will, I want us to be together, but if I could get a job like nursing I would have to seem to be unattached. It's bloody unfair! Will, I have to ask you, and please give me an honest answer, how would you feel about me doing a job away from home and probably having to live some distance away from you?"

Will replied, "I want you to do whatever you think is best for yourself. I just have to cope with you being away as best I can."

"Thank you, Will. You're a lovely man. I'll see how often I can get leave or slip away so that we can stay together as much as possible. I don't want to lose you. Can you cope with all this Will? Please be straight with me."

Will's mind was whirling with all these potential changes in his life and wondering if he could stay single without the comforts of Mary.

"Joe and I earn enough at present to keep up with the rent. But I will miss you and hope you are not going to be away for too long an interval. I love you Mary Badman." There! He realised he'd said it and waited for Mary's response.

"I love you too, Will. Thanks. I won't forget you. Please don't forget me."

Mary had asked herself where was the best place to get started in nursing? She concluded that it would be the very place most people would dread going anywhere near – the workhouse. They would have to have nurses there, of a sort. She needed to find out if it was a good idea to get some experience there first, before trying for a hospital job.

Mary took herself to the big workhouse at Mile End.

She reckoned it was a safe distance from where she lived so perhaps no one would know her there. The workhouse was a large building in Bancroft Road, with a school attached to it. She rang the front door at the porter's lodge. The porter opened the door and in a pleasant, gentle manner, asked how he could help.

"Are there any vacancies for a nurse in the workhouse?" asked Mary.

"You're in luck, my dear," he replied, "I've just put up this notice. See, here it says the Board of Guardians want to appoint a nurse for the female infirmary and sick ward. The person to be appointed has to be single or a widow, aged between 25 and 40. The salary would be twenty pounds a year, with lodging provided by the workhouse."

"Lucky me," replied Mary, "I just make it in terms of my age [untrue she told herself]. How do I apply? And may I ask your name?"

"My name is Mr Parsons, John Parsons. Listen, miss, you'll have to put your skates on. The next meeting of the Board will be in a week's time. If you want the position, I would advise you to write a letter as soon as possible to the Chairman of the Board. He will want to know your age, any previous occupations and why you want to work here."

"Thank you, Mr Parsons," said a smiling Mary.

On the day of the interview, the matron, Mrs Fox, gave her a tour of the place. They went through room after room, each one being for a separate category of inmates.

"These are the rooms where we put the elderly," said Mrs Fox. "There are more of them here than any other group of residents. They'll take up much of your time here, if you get the job."

Mary did not detect much sympathy in the voice of Mrs Fox for those who had no choice but to end their lives in sparse, cold dormitories with nothing to call their own. She was a fussy, domineering kind of person whose kinder side, if she ever had any, had long since drained away. "Been here over twenty years so there's not much that escapes me and that includes what the staff get up to," she said, giving Mary a suspicious look.

"This here is where we put the widowed women, the spinsters and those fallen women who have young children."

Under her breath Mary was thinking, "It's hardly a woman's fault if a man leaves her holding his kids. Not everybody gets legally married." She was quietly thinking of her ties to Will.

"The babies are a darned nuisance and an extra cost. At least once the children are able to walk, they will be separated from their mothers and taken to the school building where the orphans and other children are kept."

"How often do women condemn their own kind," thought Mary. They moved onto the sections where the men were placed. There was one for able-bodied men and one for the deaf and dumb and blind. "Get tired of shouting at them," said Mrs Fox, "but they never seem to take a blind bit of notice. Ha! that was almost funny.

"Down the end of that long corridor is where we put the maddun's. Obviously they're kept under lock and key. I'm not taking you there now. It's a secure unit and we don't want them getting disturbed by our presence. You'll stay out of there unless some emergency happens."

Mary next met the medical officer who would be her immediate boss. His name was Robert Thomson. To Mary's polite, "Good morning, Mr Thomson," he replied, "You are to address me as Doctor Thomson, if you please. Now then, can you read? I shall be writing down directions on the diet and treatment for different patients. I expect you and the other nurse, McClay, to carry out my instructions and not bother me unnecessarily." And that was that.

Mary subsequently found that there was no evidence of Mr Thomson having been actually trained at a medical school.

Then came the interview with the master of the workhouse and his wife, Mr and Mrs Fox. "I expect everyone to pull their weight," Mr Fox said with the air of someone who felt he was fortunate to have been trusted by his Board of Guardians with a very important and responsible duty. "Always remember, Miss Badman, that it is the ratepayers who pay for the institution and our wages. Your top priority, above all else, is to observe the need to economise and save money whenever and wherever possible."

Mary was appointed without further testing or questioning. She began working immediately. She was introduced to her new colleague, Susan McClay. Susan came from Glasgow. Mary and Susan got on well together. They knew their priority was to try to maintain high standards of cleanliness. All the inmates' clothes were to be regularly changed, leaving the inmates to wash themselves, if they were capable. They worked closely with the laundry supervisor, handling the large volume of bedding which needed cleaning. The last member of their team was the supervisor who cooked the meals.

The workhouse-master's wife seemed to be a timid woman when she was with the master. It soon became obvious however that whenever the master was not around, she would always be criticising the staff or spying on them in order to have something to complain about to her husband.

Poor Susan was frightened of her more than the master. As a result, it was Susan who got picked on more than Mary because Mrs Fox could detect that Susan could be intimidated. One of Mrs Fox's standard complaints was to criticise Susan for over-zealous changing of sheets, the cost of cleaning of which the workhouse would have to bear. Conscientious Susan bore the complaint instead of arguing that sheets had to be constantly changed for obvious reasons.

Mrs Fox's words, "The master will have to hear about this," were enough to send Susan into a state of anxiety.

"Don't worry," Mary told her, "It's just the mistress's way of trying to look important. Her bullying shows she's a coward underneath." Mary herself was finding Mr

Thomson more difficult to handle. She suspected that he realised he could not fool her and that made him even more obnoxious.

For some months, Mary stuck at the job. But by May the next year she had had enough. No matter how kind or helpful she tried to be, she couldn't put out of her mind the fact that all the people in the workhouse were there because they had to be. There was resentment and anger, as well as desperation. It was a prison.

The work required of the men was the same as that done by prisoners – stone-breaking and oakum picking. Then there were the unmarried mothers, many of whom were ex-prostitutes or addicted to drugs or alcohol. What made it worse was that many of the women were also young. They were unhappy; felt rejected and seemed to be without hope.

Mary came to the decision that she could do little to help these unfortunate people in a place like the workhouse. She also needed more opportunities for training than the workhouse could offer.

Her next move many would have considered a way of signing her own death warrant. She applied for a job in a new smallpox hospital in Plaistow. A smallpox hospital had been opened up well away from the crowded houses in the southern part of West Ham. Outbreaks of smallpox had been so frequent in the area of the Thames and the River Lea that the Board of Guardians felt they had to do something.

After she had applied to be a nurse, Mary was called for an interview. This interview was a serious test of her suitability for the position.

A medical man – she assumed he was a doctor – was asking the questions. After the usual ones about her name, address and where she had worked before, he asked her age.

"Twenty-two," she said.

"I have to ask this, my dear," he said, "because we reckon that by the age of twenty or so, if you've survived the usual range of illnesses and diseases that kill many young people, then you've probably got a pretty strong constitution. Our nurses have to be fit and strong to lessen the chances of them going down with infection here. I take it you are aware of the risk you are taking?" Mary replied that she was.

"Have you been vaccinated against smallpox?" he next asked.

"Yes, sir. Back in Somerset where I originally came from, the local vestry made us all be vaccinated against smallpox," Mary said.

"Very good. Now one of your duties is to administer medications. Please look at the label on this bottle – what does it say?" The doctor leaned forward and gave her a brown bottle. The liquid inside looked clear.

"The label says "carbolic acid, sir" Mary said.

"Have you any idea what uses it can have?"

"I think it is good for cleaning and destroying germs," she replied.

"Good. Yes, it is used for sterilising. All the walls and floors must be regularly scrubbed thoroughly with carbolic acid. Could it ever be swallowed?"

"No, sir, I'd think that could be dangerous."

"Well, in a diluted form, people use it for gargling. But, in its undiluted form, a few spoonfuls would be fatal. This bottle should always be kept separate from all other medicine bottles and under lock and key. Now tell me about this bottle."

Mary looked at the second bottle and said, "I know this one sir. It's laudanum. There were women in the workhouse where I worked who had become addicted to it."

"Well, yes, if people get hold of too much, it can be the ruin of them. But it can be useful in treating inflamed joints and for sending people to sleep. We do have bottles of morphine in the dispensary but you must never go into there unless instructed. We do not want any of our nurses either killing themselves or wanting to try opium. Now a third bottle for you to read out to me."

It was a dark liquid inside, the colour of which she could not judge through the brown bottle. "It says "potassium permanganate", sir," she said.

"Any idea of its use?"

"No, sir, I haven't," Mary replied.

"I wouldn't expect you to at this early stage," said the doctor, "we use it to wash out the mouth and throats of our patients. It also helps to stop persistent itching. You'll use it a lot.

"Well, thank you Miss Badman. I shall report to the matron that you seem sensible enough and that I'm sure you will be suitable. But you will have to be vigilant and not take risks with your own health." The doctor smiled.

"Thank you, sir. I'll do my best to look after myself as well as the patients."

The interview was over. Clearly if the doctor was satisfied that Mary would be able to cope, the rest seemed easy.

Mary was put under the supervision of Sister Buxton. The first time she walked onto the ward the first thing which struck her was the darkness. "You'll have to get used to working in the dark here, Nurse Badman. We have to draw the curtains across the windows to try to protect our patients' eyes from too much light."

Sister Buxton turned to Mary and noticed the slight shiver that went through her body. "And that's another thing you'll have to adjust to. The windows have to be kept open to help ventilation. It's sometimes very cold on the ward, especially in winter when icicles hang from the window handles. The other thing you'll have to get used to is being on your knees scrubbing floors, and washing walls and anywhere else you can think of that I might inspect every day. If there's one thing I always insist on it is perfect cleanliness at all times to offset the danger of any nasty little bugs thriving on my ward."

"How many patients on average have to be admitted each day?" asked Mary.

"It varies. Some days it's one or two, other days it's over ten."

"Where do they come from?" asked Mary

"Some are the sailors who've arrived in the docks from all over the world. Then there are the many who live locally in homes which lack fresh air and proper sanitation. All I do know is that from our point of view there's a constant stream of people brought in to be treated. Now, that's enough questions. I'm assigning you to work with Nurse Morrison. She's been here over six months and will help you get used to things."

Nurse Morrison was some years older than Mary. She was pleasant and asked Mary her first name. Then she went on to say, "Mine's Jenny. I think it would be a good idea if we work together on the next new patient on the ward. That way you can adopt the patient and see him or her through until either they recover or more likely die, I'm afraid. You see we only get to meet our patients once the disease has been diagnosed."

Within a few minutes Mary had her first patient. A middle-aged man shuffled onto the ward and was met by the sister who brought him over to Mary and Jenny. "The name we've got for this man is Mehmet. We think he's Turkish. I'll assign him a bed so you can deal with him."

Just one look at Mehmet in his worn, dirty clothing was enough to set the nurses into action. "Mehmet, I want you to take off all your clothes immediately," said Jenny. Mehmet's eyes registered confusion. "Your clothes, off!" repeated Jenny, tugging at his greasy shirt to indicate what she expected. Now he understood. "No, no," he said.

"We have to do this to all new patients," said Jenny to Mary. "Their clothing is bound to carry the infection. If Mehmet can't speak much English, it just makes our work more difficult.

"Come along, Mehmet, we can't stay around doing nothing." Then, turning to Mary, in an aside voice, she said, "some men can't cope with undressing in front of strange women. But if we have to, we'll drag them off him."

Back to Mehmet, she said, "I want them all off. Now! Don't worry about us or anybody else. The other patients won't look at you and we've seen it all before."

It became a struggle but it was obvious the nurses were going to win, if only because Mehmet was already suffering from pains all over his body and high fever. Off came his shirt, then his trousers. He had no underpants so he tried to cover his genitalia before jumping into the bed allocated to him as fast as possible. He was clearly distressed. Jenny did her best to make him comfortable. She turned to Mary and said, "Take these away and dump them in the basket by the door. All clothing is always taken away and burnt."

"How long has he been infected, do you reckon?" asked Mary.

"About a fortnight, I'd say. By now, the virus has managed to spread throughout his bloodstream, multiplying and swarming as it goes. Did you notice the rashes which were starting to appear on his skin? It won't be long before those rashes become the familiar pock marks."

Mary settled down to a daily series of rituals. Since everything the patient touched or breathed on continued to house the virus, bedding was constantly being changed and all surfaces were doused in carbolic. As for the patients, Mary got used to having to rush to the patients' side when they were screaming in agony and trying to tear off their own flesh. Sometimes she was allowed to administer small doses of laudanum if a doctor agreed it would help a patient sleep. She also had to become accustomed to the appalling smell of rotting flesh.

Meanwhile pock marks were starting to emerge from under the surface of Mehmet's skin. They began swelling up and spreading all over his body. Worst affected was his face which became so swollen that his eyes were unable to open. He was also unable to breathe. Mary had already learnt that this was the stage when the struggle to survive was really on. It was a race between the time the virus took to run its course and the body's ability to hold out against a major organ failure.

After a week, the pustules of pus ruptured, discharging their virus-laden contents. From now on, Mehmet would spend hours alert but in excruciating pain. An itching sensation caused him to scream with agony and discomfort. At other times he fell into a delirium, whilst moaning remorselessly. His breathing deteriorated. His lungs were probably under attack. He developed mouth ulcers which she tried to clean out with the potassium permanganate she had first heard of at her interview. Then she applied a cold compress on his face and eyes and gave him light food to eat. Sometimes he was partially conscious. Now and then, he whispered the word *tesekkurler* which Mary did not understand, till after a few occasions, she realised meant something like 'thank you'. As the pustules dried out, they became scabs. The itchiness this caused was a new source of discomfort to him. But by then his body and lungs were ready to give up the ghost.

Mehmet died as merciful a death as he could wish in his circumstances. In his case it was pneumonia. His lungs, already weakened by the disease, could not cope with the cold environment of the hospital ward. Mary, who had gone to his bedside at every spare moment she could grab, saw her first patient depart in peace. There was no room for sentiment as his body was swiftly removed for burial. As his body was taken away, Mary got to wondering whether Mehmet had a wife or family back home and how they would ever get to know his fate, dying alone and in a faraway country.

Every day these personal tragedies repeated themselves. What distressed Mary most at first was the death of those pregnant women who died in childbirth. The only merciful death was reserved for the very old and the very young who died from pneumonia or pleurisy. There were a few survivors. Generally they were young, or perhaps they already had a degree of resistance within their immune system.

Now and again Mary looked at her hands, once so youthful but now reddened and sore due to their constant immersion in antiseptic water. The work was laborious and physically draining. It was in these moments of exhaustion, surrounded by constant suffering and death that depressing thoughts wormed their way into her mind. "Why am I doing this? Just think," she said to herself, "I could be at home now, with Will. Is he still missing me? Does he still love me? Has he got a new woman?"

CHAPTER 8

Joys and Sorrows

Monthly days off were most welcome. Mary used to tell her employer she was going home to her relatives. Whenever she arrived back in Charlotte Street, Mary would throw herself into Will's arms. "Oh Will, I'm so exhausted. 15 hours a day for days on end. I just want to sleep and forget about people dying horrible deaths. I'm so happy to be back here with you. Have you missed me?"

They would kiss and hold each other in a long embrace. Will was never quite sure how to answer the question about missing Mary. Sometimes he just said, "loads." Another time he said, "This time I'm not sure I'll let you go back." He then had to reassure Mary he was only kidding. He knew the best reply was, "I'm so glad to see you. I think your absences make me love you even more." Mary would invariably give Will another kiss and repeat the same sentiment of love.

Another remark he found himself making was, "I keep worrying you might get the disease yourself."

"So far, so good," Mary would say. Soon after she would say, "Now Will, I want a drink and then a cuddle before collapsing."

Soon after, they would be upstairs (they had the whole house to themselves nowadays) holding each other in a tight embrace and kissing passionately. Will sometimes made Mary laugh when he fell over in his haste to remove his heavy shoes. They could generally rely on Joe not being back till late after spending an evening out dancing, his favourite activity after work. Besides, Will and Mary spending the night together would not bother him in the least.

It was no surprise when eventually Mary became pregnant. She felt it necessary to leave her post before her pregnancy became apparent, but there was also a concern not to jeopardise the health of her child-to-be.

"I liked working and having my own money, though us nurses had few opportunities to spend it," Mary said. "I've been putting a little aside each week in this jar."

"I'll hide the jar away under the floorboards upstairs if you want," said Will.

"Yes please, Will," Mary replied, "From now on, we'll only have your wages to live on."

"Yes," said Will, "but we'll still be better off than those coping with large families and only casual work. We'll be alright. I'm just excited, like you are, at the idea of having our own child."

"Oh, I love you Will," said Mary, throwing her arms round him. He responded by clutching Mary tight.

"Be careful, Will, you're squeezing our little one. If it's a boy, do you want him to be called William or James or some other family name?"

"And if it's a girl, what then?" asked Will.

"Oh, I don't know. But I'm sure it's a boy."

Mary's prediction proved correct. Will asked if the baby could be named James. "The same as your dad?" asked Mary. You surprise me."

"Well, maybe I'm just following family tradition but I like the name, in spite of it being the same as my dad," replied Will.

"I'm agreeable to that," replied Mary. "I'm going to nickname him Jamie."

However it became obvious within weeks that Jamie was a sickly child, unable to breathe easily. Mary took advantage of her work at Plaistow Hospital to ask the kindly doctor who had interviewed her for the nursing post if he would see this baby boy she was looking after for a relative. (She still felt the need to be cautious about having a child of her own, in case she wanted her old job back). He agreed to a special appointment early one morning before his rounds.

Shaking his head, he said, "I'm afraid there's clearly something wrong with the child's lungs. His air tubes aren't letting enough oxygen into his lungs. Furthermore his poor breathing is putting pressure on his heart."

"Is there anything that can be done?" asked Mary.

"All I can suggest is that you try to see a specialist in The London Hospital who deals with respiratory conditions.

He might be able to treat him, but there's no cure I'm afraid. Where does the boy live, may I ask?" On being informed that the boy lived in Tidal Basin, in West Ham's Docks, he shook his head again. "The damp air and the heavy smog which I've heard about in that neighbourhood are probably aggravating his condition."

Will and Mary couldn't afford to see a specialist, nor could they realistically think about moving. They would have to do the best they could themselves for poor Jamie. Mary used to sing to him. She made him a small dog out of an old shawl, stuffed with feathers and with little eyes and a mouth knitted on its face. Jamie loved stroking and gurgling at his special friend. When he was a little older, she gave him an old slate board and chalks to keep him occupied. That way he stayed calm.

Changes in temperature affected him, but winter was always the worst season. The cold and damp triggered the coughing and the congested state of his lungs. Keeping Jamie well buttoned in a warm coat so as not to expose his chest – that was always important.

His attacks were often worse at night. His chest would start to wheeze and he was gasping for breath. He got so distressed, not understanding what was happening. Mary would do her best by cuddling him while at the same time trying not to show how upset she was that she could do nothing for him. His attacks were often very frightening. Will and Mary were scared he would peg it there and then.

Fearful that he would die young, Mary decided they

should try for another child. Within the year another son was born whom Mary wanted to call Frank. He was a healthy baby. Mary placed the baby in a cot in front of the chair where Jamie sat. Jamie would gaze upon his brother. It seemed to make him happier.

Jamie didn't make it as far as his fourth birthday. A sudden drop in temperature in November 1878 caused Jamie to catch a severe cold. All he could do was sit in a chair all day, unable to move or breathe. He could only drink warm tea. He became tearful and quiet, hardly speaking. The look of sadness in his eyes almost broke Mary's heart. His final moments came a week later when after one last gasping breath, he just quietly slipped away.

For one of the few times in her life Mary lost her self-control and began wailing and moaning so loudly the sound penetrated next door. Jane rushed in and held Mary tight while they looked helplessly at the crumpled figure to whom fate had been so unkind. "God is love. Jamie's suffering is over," Jane whispered. "God has called Jamie back to him."

Frank was standing there confused. He had never seen his mother so upset. Jane had taken him by the hand back to her house, though Frank did not want to leave his mother. Knowing Jamie was very unwell, Will came home early. In a flash, he remembered what his father had once told him about witnessing his mum's death as a young boy.

"We should all be together at this moment," said Will. "We shouldn't be afraid of death." So Frank, Mary and himself had stood around the small body of Jamie, shedding tears as they all held each other tight. "Where was God's love?" thought Will to himself.

When he was old enough, Frank enjoyed playing with Frederick and Jane Horth's children. Emma, the eldest, sometimes joined them. Monday was the favourite play day. It was clothes washing day and all the kids got involved. Their best plaything was the huge clothes mangle in the back yard of each other's houses.

One particular Monday Will and Joe had come home for a short breather from lugging coal. When they opened the door of the house, Mary called from inside the house saying, "Come out the back quickly. I want you to see something."

"Look after the horse and cart for me a moment, will you Joe?" Will asked,

"I'll stay here and keep watch in case anybody tries to nick any of our coal," said Joe.

When he reached the back yard, Will saw what the children were up to. Under the supervision of Jane and Emma (the eldest child), the children were standing around the washing mangle, giving each other the chance to take turns at various activities. Two of them would try to turn the handle of the mangle, another fed the clothes in, opening the clothes up as they got nearer to the press. Finally there was the job of "catching" the clothes after they had gone through, making sure they landed in the tin bath, not on the ground. While this was going on, the kids were singing:

Tommy by a mighty wangle
Pushed his sister through the mangle.
Mother cried in tones so bitter
Now her clothes will never fit her.

Soon after, they broke into another little ditty:

The lightning roared, the thunder flashed
And all the world was shaken.
The little pig with the curly tail
Ran out to save his bacon.

Both Mary and Will burst out laughing seeing all the youngsters so happy. "Look at little Frank trying to help out where he can," said Will. "He can't turn the handle, but he's good at stopping the clothes touching the ground."

"It's a lovely sight, but I can't stop thinking of our Jamie," said Mary. "How he would have loved to be able to play with other children but couldn't."

Frank had liked going to South Hallsville Board School. Every day he came home, bubbling with excitement. "Mum, I can say my six times table."

"Tell me then," said Mary.

Frank rattled off the first few but needed a little help with nine times six and twelve times. "Teacher says we'll try the seven times table next. She said it was more difficult but I don't mind."

"Have you made lots of friends at school?" asked Mary.

"Yes, but I like some more than others. Some try to bully you so I try to keep away from them."

"Since you've been a good boy, I got a little surprise for you. Now close your eyes. Mary delved inside a cupboard, picked up a board and some round objects. "Now you can open your eyes. Look what I've got for you."

"Gosh, mum, it's a slate board. And you've got some chalk. Can I practise handwriting like we do at school?" I can almost write my name. Can I show you?"

"What I want you to do is this. Whatever you learn at school, come home and see if you can do as good at home as you did at school. That way you'll get better quicker. I'm sure you'll do your best in your monthly tests but you need to work hard and keep practising."

"Our teacher said that if we do well at next month's test, some of us will be able to start a new subject. I think it's History," said an excited Frank.

Meanwhile Mary kept her thoughts to herself as to the original user of the slate board.

Will's mum always took a great interest in her grandchildren. She enjoyed the occasions, usually every month or so, when Will, Mary and the boys came round. The first time they all went there after Jamie's death, mum revealed to Mary that many years previously she had lost a baby girl through sickness. "It still leaves a hole in my heart to this day. You don't talk about it but it's there. You have to just get on with life and look after those that do survive, don't you?"

Mary never saw Will's dad and reckoned Will arranged their visits to try to make sure she never did. "You're ashamed of your dad, aren't you?" asked Mary.

Yes, I suppose so," replied Will. "I don't like my dad and want to avoid him as much as possible. Besides he's not interested in kids, our own included. He probably thinks, 'just another mouth to feed'. And if he gave them any kind of present, it would be something he'd nicked. No, thank you." These visits passed enjoyably enough but the shadow of his dad prevented Will from being completely relaxed.

Then came the time when, out of the blue, Will's mother said, "Your dad's given up dealing with stolen goods in the East End. Things were getting too hot for him there. He's always known when it was best to scarper and head for cover. He's gone back to his old hideouts in Essex. So I see even less of him than I did before. He manages to pass the rent money over, giving it to your brother Harry."

"Don't you get lonely at all?" asked Mary.

"Not for a second," replied mum. "No, I'm better off without him. As long as he pays the rent, I'm happy enough."

From then on, it seemed that on each visit something else had gone badly for dad. "Your dad's getting careless as he's getting older," said mum. "He was caught and convicted of trespassing on a private road whilst going after and killing a wild duck. He's been fined seven and sixpence with five shillings costs."

"Why didn't you tell us?" Will asked.

"What's the point?" replied his mother.

Later in the same year mum said to Will, "Your dad's been up before the Assizes at Saffron Walden, charged with stealing two hens and four duck eggs. He got a real shock when he was sentenced to twenty-one days hard labour."

Will's attitude changed. Maybe his dad as well as his mum needed support. Maybe his dad's day of reckoning had finally come to pass. Was reconciliation possible between them? When he knew his dad was out of prison, he paid another visit to his mum's. This time his dad was there as well. "Something in your dad's head has cracked," said mum.

Dad looked dreadful. He no longer tried to look smart. His clothing was filthy. He looked old and in a mess. He laid on a makeshift bed, muttering away to himself.

"His muttering sounds gibberish to me," said Will. "What's he trying to say?"

"When I can understand him," his mum replied, "he seems to be going on about being a jailbird, 'just like my brother many years earlier.' Whenever he's moaning about being a jailbird, I tell him straight that he's been lucky. Given all the crimes he's committed throughout his life, he could have been hanged twice over. I have to tell you if ever he walks round the house and sees Pentonville Prison outside his back window, it makes him freeze with terror."

The next time Will called, his dad was not there. "Your dad's taken himself into the workhouse in Stoke Newington. He told me he was going to lie his way in and claim to be a widower." Will gave his mum an embrace. Tears were in her eyes. "I don't know why I'm crying. He was so handsome once, now he's gone 'gaga.' I loved him once but it's sad to see him like he is now. Will you visit him, Will? Somehow he seems to think you're closer to him than his other sons, I don't know why. Perhaps it's because he knows you to be so different from him. Maybe he looks at you and wonders whether he should have lived differently. He always blamed others for becoming bad."

"Where did he say he was going to go?" asked Will.

"To the one in Mile End. He hoped nobody would recognise him there."

Will knew all about that workhouse from Mary's days working there. When he got there one evening, he was surprised to be taken to the 'insane wing' by the same Mrs Fox whom Mary had said was the wife of the workhouse master. Will found it a distressing place. Some inmates were over-excited by Will's presence among them, wanting to touch him. Others were quietly moaning to themselves. The atmosphere was overwhelmingly one of sadness and suffering. Mrs Fox took him to a corner in one of the secure areas. "That's him," said Mrs Fox. Her tone was such that Will imagined she was referring to something less than a human being. Will could scarce recognise his dad, all rolled up in a bed, helpless and quivering. Will sat down beside him.

At that moment, his father rolled his eyes and caught those of his son. He suddenly seized his arm and said, in a soft, mumbling voice, "My boy." He then began to sob.

"What would my mum say if she saw me like this? Or my dad? I've let them down badly." At this point James stopped and let out a deep sigh before continuing. "She was the one who kept us together. Knitted wonderful clothes. See this old scarf I'm wearing? She knitted that. I want it buried with me when I die."

"I'll make sure that happens, Dad," replied Will.

James spoke no more, but continued to grip his son's arm. They stayed like that until Mrs Fox, who had been standing there impatiently, asked Will to leave so as not to disturb the inmates further. "Bye, Dad," whispered Will as he left.

CHAPTER 9

Getting Carried Away

Mary had been enjoying watching her son Frank growing up. At the same time she also felt she had to go back to nursing. The hospital where Mary really wanted to be employed was the London Hospital in Whitechapel. It had its own school of nursing, based on the principles of Florence Nightingale. "I'm going to apply to get into that school," Mary declared when Frank was seven.

Except that who would look after Frank in the daytime? She talked things over with Jane next door. Her answer was immediate. "If Will can't do it, I'll see Frank gets off to school and bring him home and give him some tea till Will gets home."

"Are you sure you don't mind?" asked Mary.

"Not at all," replied Jane. "Frank gets on well with my kids. Besides your nursing is important to you and it's a worthwhile thing to do."

Mary then had to worry about Will's reaction to her going back to work. "I think I'm going to find it harder than last time you went away," Will said. "The three of us have been getting on famously together. It'll be tough for you, I reckon, leaving Frank. But I'm sure we'll all cope as best we can."

Inside, even as he was saying these words, Will had not been so sure how well he would manage being alone again. Mary replied, "There'll come a time when we can look forward to many more years in each other's company. You haven't lost me."

Will could understand why Mary wanted to be a nurse at the 'London'. It was already well-known that the 'London' would treat anybody, except incurables, and that it accepted both the sick and the poor. The motto of its famous matron, Miss Eva Luckes* was, "Patients come first."

Mary was accepted on the strength of her previous experience and the severe shortage of nurses caused by the hospital's rapid expansion in size. At her interview it was made clear to Mary that the matron was only interested in women prepared to make nursing their profession. After fourteen-hour shifts spent on the wards, nurses were required to attend evening lectures given by the medical staff. After two years' probation Mary would become a staff nurse. During her second year she was assigned to the reception area for 'accidentals' where anything could and did happen on a daily basis.

Throughout all this time she had to try to keep thoughts about Will out of her mind. She missed him so much and in particular she disliked having to deny his existence to other staff. For many of the nurses, this was to be their only life. A few dreamt of attracting a doctor who would offer to marry them. Mary was still not convinced that that was the only or best solution for women. She might gain security and the chance to have children but she would also have to accept the idea of being the 'property' of her husband.

The nurses were supposed to stay and live on site. Once a month they had a day off when Mary would come back to see her family. In addition, there were periods at the hospital when the number of patients admitted meant extra beds were needed so the nurses' accommodation was taken over. Some nurses, like Mary, were therefore then allowed to leave the hospital on condition they stayed nearby and could return in a hurry, if required. Mary was always ready to take the risk of being recalled because it gave her the opportunity to high-tail off back to Tidal Basin.

Her occasional visits perked Will up no end. Each time, after she left him to return to the hospital, he remained happy and cheerful all the next day. He continued to admire Mary but that did not stop him feeling lonely. He missed the comforts of a woman. He feared one day she would not come back to him. He was constantly nagged by doubts whether their relationship would survive these long periods apart. He kept saying to himself, "Will she stay with me? She's sure to find another man working in a place like the London, someone who'll be better educated than me. Is she really going to come home regularly or will she start to stay away for longer and longer until there's nothing to keep us together? Does she still love me? How can I tell? Am I a fool to keep hanging on like I do?"

Will knew this was a dangerous route to follow. Was he really going to go looking for someone else? Or was it just sex he wanted? "There are thousands of prostitutes in West Ham and all over London. I could go with one of them and no one would know – except Mary if she came home soon after I'd been with one. She'd probably be able to smell another woman's presence near me from a mile off." Talk of other women prompted Will to think of the women he could easily become infatuated with – someone like Frank's favourite teacher, Miss Fairfax. He'd gone to Hallsville School to pick up Frank one day when the Thames flooded and all the streets of Tidal Basin were awash with mud and slime. The school closed and parents were collecting their kids early. Will had seen Miss Fairfax and found her very attractive. "I could really love talking to someone educated and clever like her. I could talk to her about books – maybe I could walk her home and..and." His mind was full of what might happen when Frank tugged his arm. "Come on, dad, my feet are wet."

Will was also feeling the loss of good company around him. After work, he got into the habit of dropping into what was now his favourite local, the Hallsville Tavern. He would hope to find his friend Frederick there, but often he wasn't there. "Perhaps looking for me at the library, or he's at home with the kids," thought Will. Also not there was his work mate, Joe Badman. "Probably out dancing with his girlfriend, Kathryn." Will had to recognise he was quietly envious of Joe's good fortune – his girlfriend was much more easily available. So instead Will would chat briefly with one or two others who, like himself, worked in the docks. Then he would go home.

The only alternative he could think of to overcome his loneliness in the evenings was to go to the library. Then came the day he read a pamphlet called, "The Communist Manifesto" by Marx and Engels. He discovered the word 'socialism' and the word seemed to sum up all he felt about the need for a workers' revolution against their masters, the bosses.

One day Will saw on a lamp post a notice about a demonstration called by the Socialist Democratic Federation, which was due to be held on the forthcoming Saturday. Will decided to attend the march which started from Hyde Park. Joe and Will agreed to ask for a day off. Joe would try and see Kathryn while Will went to join the march. Will had never been to Hyde Park before so the whole trip seemed like an exciting adventure. Once he found his way there, he listened to a man called John Burns,* a powerful speaker with a Scottish accent. Will noticed the man was wearing a straw hat. He talked about the need for the workers to overthrow the current system and to confront those who were the enemies of the working class. To achieve a socialist revolution the workers must prepare for a struggle to make it happen.

Then the demonstration marched off, shouting slogans and carrying banners. Hundreds of people formed a column which moved down Park Lane before turning into Piccadilly. Will found it exhilarating being in a moving column of people, marching together side by side. They were passing through some of the poshest parts of London. The signs of the wealth, privilege and importance of the ruling class were constantly in front of their eyes. Passions became stirred, a toxic mixture of envy and anger. The marchers turned down St James's Street and into Pall Mall. As they did so, they passed a number of gentlemen's clubs. At this point people began using their banners to smash a number of the clubs' windows. Swayed by the crowd, and without giving any thought to what he was doing, Will joined in, breaking a couple of the windows at Claridges's. Parts of the crowd became intoxicated by their ability to roam the streets unmolested and do what they wanted. The marchers moved onto Regent Street and Oxford Street. Here shops were attacked and looting took place from a big fancy store.

The demonstration was getting out of hand. Will finally came to his senses. He decided it was time to leave the march to avoid being arrested. He walked straight home where he laid down on the bed to recover his breath. At that point Will remembered stories of his Uncle John who had been caught up in the country riots of 1830. He feared he was the latest in a line of Waltons who might become branded as a criminal.

Suddenly he sat up from the bed. He heard a sound below as the key to the front door was turned. A second later came the voice of Mary. "Hello, Will, are you home?"

Will rushed downstairs and flung himself into her arms. "Oh, Mary, I'm so glad to see you."

"Hold me tight for a minute, Will. I want to feel you close to me."

Following a long embrace, Mary looked up at Will and said, "I've been hearing about a violent demonstration in the West End. Something about the Socialist Democratic Federation. I hope you had nothing to do with it."

"So what are people saying about it?" asked Will.

"That the marchers went from Hyde Park and Park Lane to Piccadilly. That they smashed the windows of some gentlemen's clubs in Pall Mall and committed acts of vandalism in Regent and Oxford Streets. Will, you haven't answered my question, something you always accused your father of doing."

"Oh, Mary, you should have been there to hear our leader, John Burns. His words are so powerful he is referred to as 'a voice of thunder'. Then we marched off, shouting slogans and carrying banners. Things did get a little out of hand later, like you said."

"Were you involved in any of the smashing of windows and looting from stores? Have you been that stupid?" Mary was looking him firmly in the face.

"We were all fired up and angry. Do you realise how many people are out of work down the docks. Nobody in government, none of the bosses care about families sinking into starvation. We were standing up for those people and the sight of those fat slobs sitting in their cosy chairs, drinking their fine spirits got to me. So I used the pole of my banner to smash the windows of this club. But I never ran off with any of the clothes and other things people took – I don't want to be a thief like my father."

"You 'doughboy' Will," exclaimed Mary. "Asking for trouble. You're lucky you didn't get arrested."

"Me and some of the other marchers quickly left the march to avoid being caught. The only person who was arrested was our leader, John Burns, and he's now been let off."

"I don't often think of you as a fool, Will, but this time you were," said Mary. "I know you want to be involved in standing up for the rights of people but all this talk about socialism worries me a little, especially if this Socialist Federation goes out of its way to cause trouble.

"Oh, Will, I come home for a few hours to see you and all you do is make me annoyed and concerned as to what you'll do next while I'm not around. I want you to promise me there'll be no more smashing of windows or getting violent – and be careful about what you read. Reading can be dangerous as well."

"But Mary, the fact that I can get hold of lots of books and get more knowledge is so important to me. I'm not an educated man but I'm determined to get hold of as many good books as I can. To catch up on those who know more than me."

"Fine, Will, but don't get carried away with wild ideas about socialism."

"Mary, socialism is not a wild idea. It must happen one day."

"Will, enough of this. I want a rest and sleep. Go and make me a cup of tea and let's sit down quietly for a short while. No more politics tonight, please."

One evening after work, Will dropped into the Hallsville and was pleased to see not only Frederick but also Walter.

"Hello, Will, how are you? Still mucking about lifting tons of coal and feeding horses," were Walter's typical opening remarks.

"Yep, but it feels harder lifting those sacks as you get older. The horse is doing well, good for conversation when Joe and I get fed up with our voices," replied Will jokingly.

"Have you heard about this young man here?" said Walter turning to Frederick. "He's given up on shuttle trains."

"I work with real trains now," said Frederick, "I work for the General Eastern Railway. I'm based at the Goods Depot in Silvertown. Still maintaining trains but they're proper trains, not like the ones Walter still drives at Thames Ironworks."

"Suits me for now. Besides I don't have to look after you," said Walter nudging Frederick.

"Talking about looking after," said Will, "Mary and I

116

are most grateful, Frederick, that your Jane collects Frank from school for us. Those kids all get on well together."

"They're all doing well, thanks be to God," said Frederick.

"Emma is so lively, so much fun, I'm told," said Will.

"You know my wife and I are pretty quiet and orderly, Will. That's why Emma stands out. She's very high-spirited. There's something special about her," he said.

"She's certainly got a reputation," said Walter. "She's always getting into fights with boys because she is prepared to stand up to them. And, she seems to get away with it."

"She's obviously pretty smart getting into secondary education with my Frank," said Will.

"I know that," said Frederick, "but I just worry her risk-taking nature could land her in trouble one day."

CHAPTER 10

So Father can still surprise us

James Walton died a week after his son's visit to the workhouse. Following the usual practice for such inmates, he was quickly buried in an unmarked grave. So it was on a grey drizzly day in the autumn of 1887, that Will looked down at the earth in which the mortal remains of his father had recently been interred. It was in the corner of a burial ground in Stoke Newington, London, reserved for paupers, the old and insane. Since none of his family respected the old man during his lifetime, it was as if the memory of having had a father had disappeared from their minds. Will was the only one who had bothered to find the grave.

It was precisely at that moment that he came to the conclusion that, whether he liked it or not, he now shared something with his father – they were both law-breakers. He remembered how he had once challenged his father with the words, "Have you ever been done for breaking the law, Dad?" That argument had taken place very near where he was standing. The same question he had put to his father could now be put to the son.

Dad used to kid himself he was acting in the spirit of a famous hero and son of Essex, Dick Turpin. Turpin only robbed the rich and defied the authorities to catch him. When they did finally capture and sentence him to be hanged, Turpin died putting on a show for the assembled crowd, like a public entertainer.

Getting caught was something to be avoided. His dad had always said, "You've got to be smart and don't do anything too stupid and your luck might just last." Well, his father's luck didn't last either.

Dad liked to justify his law-breaking as an act of defiance at what life had done to him. So what was the son's excuse for smashing the windows of the gentleman's club in Pall Mall? He liked to justify his actions in the cause of socialism and revolution, though if he was honest with himself, he had to admit it was a stupid thing to do. Did he want to risk getting a criminal record like his dad?

Turning his back on the grave, Will began to walk back to his mother's home in Finsbury. He, like the rest of his brothers and sisters, had been ordered to be there this day.

When Will finally arrived at his mother's house, all the members of the family were already there. In the middle of the room was a large strongbox, the lid of which was unfastened but closed.

"We're all wondering what's inside," said Charlie, now a strapping teenager.

"Probably something nasty. I'm not sure I want to know what's there," said Alice, also no longer a child.

Their mother then made it clear she wanted to speak.

"Now you're all here, I want to tell you all something truly wonderful. Your late father always said that he would look after me when he'd gone, to make up for all the times when he either wasn't here or when the money went short. Well, believe it or not, he's kept his word."

After a pause, she added, "Charlie, I want you to lift the lid of the box on the floor."

Very gingerly, Charlie did as he'd been told. Once the lid was pushed back, everybody let out a gasp of amazement.

"I've never seen so much money in my life," exclaimed Harry.

"Whose is it?" asked Alice.

Charlie got excited running his fingers through the metal pieces. The coins, consisting of shillings, florins and half-crowns, were piled up on top of each other.

Mother continued, "Though your dad died only a short time ago, word of his death must have got out. Yesterday two total strangers, one of whom called himself Jack, came to my door with this strongbox. Jack said he was an old mate of your dad. He added that your dad had trusted him with a special mission to be carried out after his death. Your dad had told this friend of a location in Epping Forest where there was a hidden strongbox, the contents of which he wanted to pass on to his wife.

"This Jack, being both loyal and honest, an unusual friend for your dad to have, went and found this strongbox and brought it to me. It needed two of them to carry it. Inside were these coins. I've counted them up and the total amounts to nearly three hundred pounds."

"So father can still surprise us, even from his grave," said Will.

"Now, here's what I'm going to do with the money," mum continued. "All of you are going to share this money amongst yourselves."

Harry led the protests, "No, mum, it's your money. You deserve it after all this time."

But mum was resolute. "The money's not for you – it's for your children and their future education – use it that way. Don't you dare spend it on yourselves."

The protests continued. Cries of "no, it's not right" were heard. Harry then spoke for all of them,

"Mother, we insist that you keep some for yourself. At least twenty pounds for your own comfort. That will enable you to buy some new curtains and a comfy chair."

Everybody nodded in agreement and mother gave way. Harry and John began dividing up the pile of loose change and distributing it equally to each brother and sister. Will argued his only son had just left school so he didn't need any. Mother stepped in again. "He's a bright boy. You once told me he wanted to become a teacher one day. Well, he'll need money for that."

The family gathering having ended, they all stuffed the money in their trousers, socks, jackets and anything else they could think of. A strange sight they appeared, all with bulging clothing.

As he walked home Will got to thinking what a momentous day it had been. From the unexpected feelings of grief at the death of his father, beside whose grave he had been standing only hours earlier, now he was walking back to Tidal Basin with his pockets loaded with his father's inheritance. Even if the money was illegally obtained, it could not be returned. One day it would be put to great use.

Will had to conclude that his dad was a caring man who loved his children but he didn't know how to relate to them. Perhaps only he of all his dad's children had ever got close to him, though even that was limited.

His dad had lived the life of a sewer rat, forever lurking in the shadows. In the end his life had been miserable, a lost soul with no clear sense of himself or where he belonged. No satisfactions. No use to anyone. His conscience would have told him he had missed his way in life. He could argue it was not his fault, he was the victim of circumstances. Nevertheless, was 'playing the victim,' a cover for his own weakness in taking responsibility for what he had done with his life?

By the time Will got back to Charlotte Street, it was early evening and getting dark, or 'dimpsey' as his Mary called it. Just before Will reached his front door, Jane Horth, popped open her door. "'Ev'ning Will," she said, "if you're looking for Frank he's in here with Emma and my kids. They've got together to talk about the jobs they might do now they've left school. Sounding proper grown-up they are."

"As far as I know Frank's going for casual work in a warehouse. That's not what he wants to do but he's no choice. What is Emma thinking of doing, do you know?"

Jane replied, "She reckons she'll have to do factory work somewhere, though she's doing cleaning jobs at present. Somehow I don't expect her to hang around here for long – too lively that one for her own or her father's good."

"OK, Jane, I'm going in. Just tell Frank I'll try and make him some tea when he comes back," said Will.

"Don't worry about that, Will. I'll feed him along with the rest."

"Thanks Jane, you're a brick. Don't know how we'd have got along without you, Mary and I, all these years."

"That's what neighbours are for, Will. Help each other along."

Will turned the key of the front door. As he did so he could hear the sound of movements inside the front parlour.

"Hello, Will, how's the afternoon gone?" The voice was that of Joe Badman.

"Tell you what. I've got quite a story to tell you, Joe," replied Will. "Hello, Kathryn, hope I haven't disturbed you lovers by my arrival."

"That's alright, Will," said Kathryn, "we heard you talking to Jane. Joe finally let me off his knee."

"Cheeky woman, you are," said Joe. "Anyway we're off to a dance at the Hack Hall."

"You two and your dancing. No wonder you both get on like a house on fire and have done ever since you went out together," said Will.

"It's good for your love-life," said Joe, "all that close contact with each other."

"Give over, Joe, You're embarrassing me," said Kathryn.

"So, what's your big story then, Will?" asked Joe.

"Let's have a cup of tea first," said Kathryn. "We've got time before we go out. She strolled out of the room and seconds later could be heard the sounds of the copper being placed on the range fire.

"Come on then, out with it Will," said Joe a few minutes later, full of expectancy.

When Will had finished, Joe's first response was to say, "You'll have to hide that money somewhere upstairs, to be safe. Under the floorboards would probably be best."

Will took Joe's advice and went upstairs to the room he shared with Mary. First he pulled back the mattress on the floor. Then, using a penknife he raised the floorboard, put the coins inside an old pair of leather boots to keep out the dampness and the mice, before replacing the board and the old mattress. A quick look for any fleas and bedbugs revealed that Mary had recently had a go at cleaning all round the floor area.

Joe called up to say he and Kathryn were off. Will was now alone in the house. He lit the paraffin lamp before stretching out on the bed. The feeling of loneliness quickly overcame him again. The only solution he could think of was to get even more involved in political meetings. These he would attend as often as he could.

Word quickly spread when well-known speakers would be at a meeting. Hundreds of men would gather to hear the likes of John Burns, Will Thorne* and Ben Tillett.* What Will found particularly inspiring was that the three men were happy to admit they were self-educated, like he was trying to be. They may not have been able to write but they could stand up and make speeches. They openly talked about socialism and the need for the workers to organise trade unions for each of their trades and occupations.

In November 1887, there was a second demonstration by the Socialist Federation which Will was determined to attend. He had just kept quiet about the forthcoming event when he had seen Mary.

The plan had been for the marchers to meet up with marshals at a pre-arranged street near Trafalgar Square. When Will arrived, banners were being handed out. Will took one declaring, 'We Demand Jobs for All'. But the 'March of the Unemployed' as it was called, never got as far as Trafalgar Square. The police had learnt their lesson from the last demonstration, and were determined to stop the demonstration before it got underway. As the marchers moved off, intending to occupy the square, the police defended it in large numbers.

The marchers tried to break the police cordon. There was a lot of pushing and throwing of punches. Will joined in and distinctly remembered landing a punch on the jaw of an officer. The officer's retaliation was swift. A truncheon landed on Will's head. He fell to the ground. All around him were a number of injured men.

As the fighting continued, the police called up some troops on horseback who must have been already stationed in Horse Guard's Parade, waiting for the signal to advance into the crowd. Will got up, recovered his banner and joined other demonstrators in using their banners as weapons to hold back the horses. They could not hold out for long and quickly scattered.

In all the mayhem, Will had enough sense to run away and was amazed when he actually managed to reach as far as Soho before daring to stop running. Once there he was able to vanish amongst the crowd of traders, prostitutes and beggars who thronged everywhere.

"Running away, just like my dad once did," muttered Will to himself.

Will arrived back home that night and laid down to rest. He reckoned his injury would not stop him getting to work the next day. He was struggling to understand the mix of his emotions as to what had happened. On the one hand, he was thrilled to have been on the demonstration. The excitement of being amongst those fellow workers who had fought back against the police was only tempered by fear when the horses charged and overwhelmed them. The demonstration had been risky.

On the other hand, had it been worth it? Maybe it was but he was unhappy that it had been the second time that he had lost his temper and been violent.

Then he began to worry as to what others would think of his behaviour. Mary would scold him with that expression of hers – 'doughboy'. His friend Frederick would certainly not approve. And what would his dad have said? He would have called him a fool too for risking being arrested when he needn't have been involved in the first place.

When he did get to the library next evening, he read in the newspapers that hundreds had been arrested, many others were hurt and one man was killed. Among those arrested was John Burns. A well-known woman speaker called Annie Besant,* who had also been part of the demonstration, had invited the police to arrest her, but they wouldn't.

Will had indeed had a lucky escape.

CHAPTER 11

Cead Mile Failte
(A Hundred Thousand Welcomes)

One evening after work Will decided to wander off in the direction of Silvertown for a pint. As he approached a pub called the Tidal Basin Tavern, he heard loud sounds of music and laughter coming from within. He checked himself and wondered what might be going on. It was not a Friday or a Saturday when many pubs enjoyed a 'knees-up' as Cockneys called it. Furthermore the songs and the music were not familiar. Stepping inside, he quickly realised the reason for the celebration. It was St Patrick's Day, the 17th March.

Will could not understand the level of prejudice people held against the Irish. He had moved a long way in his attitude from the days when he lived in Islington where the Irish were seen as foreign and dangerous. Will knew if he went up to the respectable parts of Stratford, the Irish would still be spoken of as 'wild, drunken, and lazy,' or as 'less than human.' The police certainly held that opinion, on the basis of the number of occasions they had to restrain or arrest Irishmen.

There were many Irish families living in Tidal Basin. They usually had to live in the worst housing whilst the men struggled to find work. But they stood together and welcomed anybody into their midst if they were honest and straightforward. As far as Will was concerned they were the sort of people a man could rely on if they were on your side, but woe betides those who crossed them. And they had a great sense of humour.

That evening, as he worked his way to the bar, the first thing he had to do was to keep clear of the high-stepping dance that some fellow was performing. The music was being played on a violin and an accordion. The singing was led by another man with everybody joining in whenever they wanted.

The area surrounding the bar was four deep in men. Many moved away once they got served but those propping-up the bar moved aside to make way, if they could be persuaded to cease talking or laughing for a moment. The accents sounded very different, but as far as Will was concerned, he could hardly understand a word they were saying. It was also incredibly noisy.

Will knew that the second he opened his mouth, he would be identified as being English. At the counter two men separated for Will to order his pint of beer.

"How do?" said one of the men, "come for a bit of Irish fun have you? Don't worry, you'll be welcome here. Isn't that right, Sean?"

"Anyone who wants to enjoy a drink on St. Patrick's is alright by me," said Sean.

"Is it always like this here on St. Patrick's?" asked Will. "So many people – men, women and kids."

"Ah, yes, it's one night we forget our troubles and celebrate being Irish, have a good laugh and drink plenty, wouldn't you say, Pat?" Pat nodded.

"My name's Will," said Will. "I live not far from here."

One of the men held out his hand, "How'd you do, Will. My name is Sean."

The other man did likewise. "And I'm Pat. We're brothers."

"Do you two live in Tidal Basin?" asked Will.

"Yes, we've got lodgings in Victoria Dock Road," offered Sean.

"I was listening to the accents of people. Do the folks here come from all over Ireland?" asked Will.

"To be sure," said Pat, "from Mayo, Longford, Waterford, Dublin, all over."

"Where do you two come from?" asked Will.

"Patrick and I come from Cork, from Kinsale," replied Sean.

Right on cue it seemed, the singer invited the audience to sing any song that came from their home county. A voice in the crowd then chipped in with a song with a regular chorus that went, "You're welcome as the flowers in May in dear old Donegal."

"Well now, you know where he comes from," said Pat.

Further contributions included 'Rose of Tralee', 'Galway Bay' and 'In Dublin's fair city.' Each contribution was cheered loudly. Will offered to buy his companions a drink, which they accepted – two pints of Guinness. The two pints ordered were lined up on the counter, half full, alongside many other glasses in the same state. They were all deliberately not topped up for a couple of minutes. Once the Guinness was settled, the other half was poured in. Due to this gap in time between ordering the drink and waiting for the stout to settle, many of the drinkers ordered a fresh pint long before they had finished the previous one.

"That way we never have to stop drinking," observed Sean.

A toast was offered by Will to St Patrick and the men raised their glasses accordingly.

"How long have you been living in Tidal Basin?" asked Will.

"A couple of years in fact. Before that we were in Poplar," said Sean. "We came here to try and get work in the docks."

"And that's not easy, I can tell you," said Pat. "Do you work there?"

"I work for one of the coal yards, delivering coal," said Will. "Not as dangerous as working along the dock front."

"Ah, you can say that again," said Pat. "Many's the men who've been hit by cranes, tripped up over ropes and cables, fallen into ships' holds or drowned in the water."

"Have you had much luck getting work lately? Seems to me there's a lot of men, probably hundreds, get nothing," said Will.

"It's like playing bagatelle," started up Sean, "the odds of winning work are stacked against you. It doesn't matter how quick you are to reach the dock gates once the horns sound. You don't know whether there might be work for a day or a couple of hours. All you know is that there will be hundreds of you and that the ones certain to be called in are the 'preference' men. To become one of those you have to be a friend of the foreman – buying drinks for him or offering to pay a percentage of your wages for being selected to work."

"Some of those bastards enjoy playing tricks like throwing work tickets up in the air to watch people scrambling and fighting each other to grab one," added Pat. "I ask you now, can it be a surprise that men, without any hope of a job, desperate to feed their families, loaf about the dock gates, go about begging and stealing, hoping the dock constables don't catch 'em?"

Just at that moment a woman jostled her way to the bar and stood between Pat and Sean. "Bejesus, you'd forget your own family, yous two would, standing at the bar drinking and forgetting about Mairead and myself. Who's your friend?"

Will was introduced. Meanwhile Pat called over the barman and ordered two bottles of stout and more drinks for themselves and Will.

"You don't go talking too much about politics, the pair of yous. Keep the party friendly-like." With that the woman, who was called Marion, moved away back to her sister-in-law.

"Well, Will, what do you reckon about all this unemployment then?" asked Pat, ignoring what his wife had just said to him.

"I think it's because the bosses like to see working men forced to compete against each other for the same job," started Will. "The bosses control the number of jobs available and know there's more men than jobs. It's a great way of keeping wages as low as they can get away with."

"I think you're right there, Will. Though there's not many as say so," said Pat.

"And what would you have the working man do then to make things different?" asked Sean.

"Stick together and form a union. Demand secure jobs, better housing and safe water," said Will.

"Those all be things worth fighting for. And if you want the Irish to join the struggle, we'll be there," offered Sean. "We like a good fight for justice – we've been at it for over 700 years, fighting you English."

This conversation was carried out with all of them having to shout to each other to be heard above the communal singing. All the old favourites were coming out, one after another. There were the nostalgic ones, 'Dear Little Shamrock' and 'I'll take you home Kathleen,' then to cap the lot, 'The Wearing of the Green.' The atmosphere was intoxicating and Will found himself singing along with the rest. Will was impressed – here were people who were happy and proud to be what they were.

After several pints, Will reckoned it was time to leave. With the words, "See you again, soon," he left Sean and Pat. As he walked back up the road towards home, Will looked back on their conversation and was amazed how strong he had been in his opinion as to the need for a confrontation over working conditions in the docks.

All over the East End of London, there was anger at the way the thousands of poor and unemployed were being treated. But there was no one to lead the struggle. Then onto the scene came some powerful speakers. John Burns, following the 'Bloody Sunday' demonstration of 1887, was now well-known by all. Since his imprisonment, he got the name of 'the man with the red flag,' on account of the flag always being with him, as well as his straw hat. Then there was Ben Tillett. He worked in a tea warehouse in Tilbury. Another person Will came across was Will Thorne. Finally there was Annie Besant.

It was Annie Besant who decided to take up the struggle for a group of women in Bow who worked for a match manufacturer at the Fairfields Works. She managed to persuade the women workers to go on strike for better pay and improved working conditions. It was July 1888. Once the strike was underway, Will went down to Fairfield Road to show his solidarity with the strikers. He wanted to speak with the women on picket duty to check progress on the action.

As he approached the picket line, he suddenly said to himself, "I know one of those young women. It's Emma Horth. She's grown up and no longer a girl. What a surprise seeing her here." Nodding to the other pickets, he went straight up to Emma.

"Hello Emma, how amazing to see you."

"Didn't my father tell you? I left home to get a job here. I thought I'd be helping the family out – one less to feed and that. To make my parents feel better, I told them that once I'd earned some money, I'd come back home again."

"I bet that was a shock for your mum and dad. How did they take it?"

"Dad was more upset than Mum. You know how my dad thinks me his little treasure," Emma replied.

"Have you got somewhere to stay?" asked Will.

"Yes, one of the girls at work lets me share a bit of her floor space. It will do for now until I get settled," said Emma.

"So you don't think you will go back home when this is over?" asked Will.

"Don't know, we'll wait and see. So, what are you doing here, Mr Walton?"

"Please, Emma, you're not a child any more, doing what you're doing. From now on, please call me Will. Why I'm here? To support you lot. It's great what you're doing, standing up to your bosses like this. I hear it's a dreadful job to do, making matches."

"First thing to say is that it's dangerous. The head of the matches is made out of a substance called phosphorous. It can flare up suddenly and you can get burnt. Then the fumes, they're poisonous. To cap all that, the money's lousy. It's because we're women – the bosses think they can bully us and we'll do anything they demand of us."

"Bet, you're now wishing you hadn't got mixed up in all of this."

"Not at all. The girls are great. And they're tough as old nails. Many of them are Irish – you can't push them around for too long. And Annie Besant is a wonderful lady. She came along and told us we shouldn't put up with the situation any more. Told us to stand up for ourselves, fight back and get up the courage to go on strike. She inspired us all."

"Are you now organised in a union?" asked Will.

"Oh yes, though there isn't much in the way of strike pay. That's why we're going on a demonstration and march tomorrow, to see if any of the people of London will give some pennies to keep us going. Why don't you come along?"

"Willingly, if I can be of any help. What time and where's the route?"

"We're starting off from here around ten o'clock. We're marching down Bow Road to Mile End and then it's Aldgate and the City before coming back by Bethnal Green and Roman Road."

"Tomorrow's a Saturday. I'll talk to Joe and see if we

136

can start earlier so as to get through our quota by early afternoon. But I'll catch up with you somehow. Wait till I see your dad next. It'll give him a surprise when I tell him where I saw you. Bye for now and good luck,"

"Thanks Will. If you see my dad, tell him not to worry, will you?" said Emma.

Next day, late in the afternoon, Will managed to locate the demonstration. The sight that met his eyes was amazing. There were hundreds of marchers but there was no riot. The women walked in orderly ranks. Banners were flying, and some of the strikers shouted out slogans. However, mostly they were walking in a dignified manner, proud and upright. On the pavements, instead of hostility, were ranks of posh-looking ladies and gentlemen quietly applauding the marchers.

Perhaps the biggest banners that day were being held by members of church congregations, announcing the support of this or that church. One banner caught Will's eye in particular, saying 'Young girls in moral danger.' In their midst stood the ministers and church leaders.

As luck would have it, Will caught sight of Will Thorne. When Will went up to him, Will Thorne turned to Will and said, "The women are showing us how to do it. The march is peaceful, the strikers are walking tall and the crowds watching are on their side. That's the secret – getting the public on your side. When the men in the docks rise up, demanding better wages, as I'm sure they will, they could do worse than copy these brave women."

After finding Emma and getting hold of a bucket, Will walked beside her all the way back to Bow. He quickly then said cheerio and left the scene.

Less than a week later, the bosses at Fairfield works conceded to the women's demands. They got what they wanted – better pay, better hygiene and more safety measures. It was a few days after the news came out that Will finally got to see Frederick Horth at their favourite tavern. After telling Frederick how he'd seen and spoken to Emma, he added, "I'd be quite proud of what she's done, if I were you. Given that she's only fourteen and it was her first real job. I'm sure you were on her side as well. Lots of church people supported the strikers."

"I did not support the strike. I don't hold with the likes of Annie Besant and all this talk of revolution and class struggle."

Will bit his lip. He did not want an argument. He let the matter drop.

CHAPTER 12

The Dock Strike

Will Walton was bursting with excitement the day the dock strike came to West Ham. "This is what I've been waiting for," he said to himself, "the workers rising up to fight their employers." He threw himself into the struggle, disregarding all else. He wanted to be in the thick of it all.

It was on the 13th August 1889 that Ben Tillett,★ called on the men of the East & West India Docks to come out on strike. Their demands were simple – increased payment from five to six pence an hour and a minimum daily wage of two shillings. Soon afterwards the dock workers in the Victoria & Albert Docks joined the strike.

At this point it was only the dock workers who were involved. But within a week, with no ships being unloaded and trade virtually coming to a standstill, many of the other trades and labourers were involved. The question was would the stevedores, sailors, firemen and Will's men – the coal porters – support the strike?

Will seemed to take it on himself to get as many fellow workers as possible to join the strike. He started off around Tidal Basin. "Come on, mates, we're all in this together. We need to organise ourselves into a trade union."

"Will, do you realise what you're asking us to do? Why should we lose money over a dispute which is not directly ours?"

"If we set up a union, we all help each other, with what we can afford."

"Will, if we go on strike we'll have no money."

"Naw, I'm not giving up my hard-earned cash to anyone else. I'm not joining any union."

"And what will you do if the rest of us coalies do?" asked Will. This is a fight for better wages for all of us in the docks. You try and go it alone, you won't be popular if we win."

"Will, you're missing the point. What would we get in return for sacrificing our wages?"

"We would have to find money by other means. If we ask the ordinary people for support, I'm sure that'll help raise funds. It happened with the match girls' strike. Then we can hand out money as relief, to each man according to his needs and that of his family. We'll have to work hard at that, mind you. Still, we might find asking for money from the public is easier than asking for a pay rise from the bosses. That's the nut we have to crack – together."

Most of his workmates were eventually won over. Will was beginning to find his voice, to be persuasive.

Will went with other coalies, including Joe Badman, on visits around the East End, trying to spread the word and get as many trades as possible to join in. They went to Old Ford, to the railway coal yards at Stratford. At the entrance to the yard, the supervisors said, "You lot are not welcome here. What the dockers do is nothing to do with us." Meanwhile the workers themselves began to crowd around.

Will grabbed a ladder, climbed up above the heads of those around him and called out, "We're all involved in this dispute. Working men need to come together in solidarity with the dockers. Their struggle is our struggle – for better wages and the opportunity to support our families with jobs for all. We ask you to join us. Shall you come out on strike or not? All those not in favour, put your hand up." [No hand went up]. "All those in favour of going on strike, please show." A mass of hands went up and that was that. The men downed their shovels and walked out, straight past their bosses.

Will then led a group of men to another yard in Stratford. Here they found the gates were locked. The coalies forced the gates and entered the yard. At that point the workers inside decided to join up.

They went past a brewery. News of this marching band of men seeking to extend the strike beyond the docks was spreading fast. Representatives of the men were already outside the gate. "We have no complaint against our employer here," said one representative. "If you try to come in here to cause trouble, I warn you some of us are prepared to fight you. I'm telling you – stay away." Will and his men had no interest in that kind of struggle so they walked away.

Will offered to go and talk to the railway workers in Silvertown. He went straight to the huge goods depot. He was looking for Frederick Horth whom he felt he could speak to directly. "Why are you men not on strike? What's the matter with you?" said Will.

"Now, what me and the men do round here is up to us and it's none of your business if we wish to stay at work. You can't come down here telling us what we should do. It's not like you, Will," replied Frederick in a friendly but insistent voice.

"Look Frederick, this is one of those great moments, when something big is happening, when it is vital that all working men stay firm in the cause of justice and fairness. The struggle by the dockers is on behalf of all of us, trying to fight back against exploitation by the bosses. Surely you can see that?" said Will.

"Will, you're getting carried away. You may have decided you want to take the action you have but here we have no dispute with our employer," said Frederick. "You know it's not my way of doing things to go on strike. There are other ways of working to improve society. Better steady, slow steps than these big gestures."

Frederick continued, "What about the severe hardship the strike is causing to the women and families of those on strike? Are you sure you're right in what you're doing when others will suffer even more than they were doing before? Suppose you lose, what then? You'll all be worse off, as well as unhappy."

Will interrupted saying, "I didn't come here to listen to all this kind of talk. There is a class struggle taking place and I know what side I'm on. You're as much working class as me. Why won't you join in the struggle? I tell you why. Because you're a reactionary, scared to lift a finger in case you get hurt. At least your daughter Emma had the guts to go and join the match girls in their strike." By now Will was angry, but it was nothing compared to Frederick's response.

"That's enough. Don't you dare talk to me about my daughter and what she's done. I won't have it. As far as I'm concerned you've overstepped the mark, Will. Now get away from here. Don't bother trying to contact me again – at all. Not till you apologise for what you've said. Get out!" Frederick waved his hand in a dismissive gesture.

Will had no alternative but to go. Deep down he knew he'd said the wrong thing but he reconciled his behaviour by thinking to himself that it was Frederick's problem, not his. He was sorry to lose a friend but if that was the way things stood, so be it. Other things were more important than loyalty to old friends if it got in the way of bigger issues. This was a time when the working classes needed to be sure who were their friends and who was against them.

Public meetings were taking place in every area on strike. Will decided to attend in order to find out what the "respectable" middle classes thought of the action. One such meeting was held in the assembly hall in Hack Road. When Will got there, the hall was packed out, with people clustered round the door or sitting on window sills. On the platform were representatives of local employers, a leader of the stevedores, and other local dignitaries. It was there that Will also ran into Pat and Shaun Brady and Joe.

The chairman was known to them. He rose to say, "This meeting has been called to show sympathy for those living in the dock district. I want to say early on, how much we admire those who have come out in sympathy for doing such a noble thing. Funds are being collected to help those suffering.

"However I have to say that in my opinion, there is no need to spread the strike into other areas. We don't want everything collapsing about our ears. Capitalism must not be threatened. Small traders, like me, should be allowed to continue their business. A universal strike would be doomed.

"I have become alarmed at remarks supposed to have been made by Mr Burns that the strike was a preliminary to greater struggles. There is no need for socialism. What we want to suggest to you, the dock labourers, is that you appoint three of your number to meet the local dock directors to resolve this dispute amicably amongst yourselves without outside interference."

As soon as he sat down, a voice from the floor called out, "The dock directors could afford to pay the sixpence per hour payment out of their profits and should do so."

Another man joined in, "London is the wealthiest city in the world and how did its wealth come? It has no coal mines, no iron ore beds, no great cotton or jute factories. London's wealth comes by the river and it is a shame that the men who contribute to the making of that wealth cannot get a fair day's wage." A great cheer went up.

To move business along, another member of the platform party rose to announce that over five hundred pounds had been collected. They wanted this money to be distributed by a special committee comprising local dignitaries and representatives of the men.

Other offers of help came from tradesmen who were prepared to distribute soup and other food supplies. A medical gentleman said he was prepared to supply strikers with free medicine. In return for this kindness, the platform party made clear what they wanted in return.

The chairman stepped in again. "We want to see direct negotiations taking place between the workers and the directors. Three local employers have already expressed their willingness to meet representatives of the workers. What we want the workers to do is to elect three of their number who would then meet the directors. This group would be invited to join representatives from the other side of the River Lea. It is hoped that by this means, all sides could combine to request arbitration to settle the dispute."

At this point, Will realised what was going on. It was a manoeuvre by the employers to keep the union out of the negotiations and to try to persuade sympathetic non-union workers to come to an agreement to settle the strike, without conceding to the unions' demands.

Fortunately, on the night, the men had not been able to agree as to who they wanted as their representatives. When the meeting ended, Will made sure to pass on the information about the local employers' tactics to the strike committee. "It's happening across the East End," he was told. "We must prevent the men from joining these separate negotiations. Let them divide and rule us, and we'll lose."

It was a great surprise to those in Tidal Basin to read in the local paper that the vicar of St Luke's had spoken from the pulpit to refer to the good understanding between the church and its parishioners, especially the wives and children. "I strongly recommend the strikers accept the concerns of the Dock Company for the vulnerable members of the dockers' families and return to work."

The Wade's Arms in Jeremiah Street, Poplar served as the Strike HQ. From the early days of the strike, it was decided that processions were an important part of keeping spirits high as well as keeping the public on their side. To avoid trouble with the police, all the delegates were instructed to insist on certain ground rules.

"The men should respect the authority of the police and the property of the dock companies," said Will Thorne, perhaps reminding John Burns that the aggressive tactics previously used by the Socialist Democratic Federation were not welcome.

"Another good idea would be to encourage the men to get hold of some of their work wagons," said Ben Tillett, "to make displays which show the range of jobs the strikers are engaged in, like carrying heavy loads."

"We could have banners and flags to wave. But no calls for revolution – you'll frighten the public," added Will Thorne.

"Let's see if some of the local brass bands would come along and play whilst the men are marching," said a delegate.

The idea of decorating a wagon appealed to Will. Joe and he quietly got hold of their work wagon and two horses. They "borrowed" their working leather hood and studded back guards, which they would wear.

"What are we going to decorate our wagon with? Slogans?" asked Joe.

"How about if we made up banners which we stretch round the sides and back of the wagon with words like… Coal Porters and Carmen – in solidarity with the Dockers," suggested Will.

"We'll have to make sure we spell that word "solidarity" properly – that's your job since you like using the dictionary so much," prompted Joe. "And how are we going to decorate the horses?"

"Stick a few lumps of coal on their heads," said Will jokingly. They both laughed and began in earnest to prepare for the march on the following day.

Custom House was the starting point for the march from the Victoria and Albert Docks. The route was along Victoria Dock Road, over the Iron Bridge and down past Poplar Hospital. There they joined other groups for a combined march down through Aldgate to the City.

From the start, the strikers were amazed to find they were being cheered all the way by members of the public. These cheers the strikers acknowledged by raising their caps. The marchers stopped when they reached the companies' Dock House in Leadenhall Street. After a few minutes of shouting and jeering, they moved off back to Aldgate and then down Commercial Road for a massed meeting. That first march there were probably sixty to seventy thousand marchers.

Processions like this made all the strikers feel ten feet tall. So they were organized on a regular basis to keep morale high. Then there were the regular meetings in the evenings. Often they included details of the donations made by the churches and individual members of the public. After the formal proceedings, free entertainment was provided by professional actors and singers from London's theatre land. "The people of London are on our side," the strikers all said.

Will was given responsibility for organising the picket rota for the coal workers in the Victoria & Albert Docks and for linking with all the other trades. Picket lines were also co-ordinated across London. An unbelievable number of around three thousand pickets were undertaking night and day shifts, starting and finishing at midday and midnight.

The main reason for the picket line was to spot non-union men (blacklegs) being brought into the docks to move the cargo which needed unloading from the ships. The strike committee issued the following instructions:

"Pickets are to try to persuade the blacklegs to stop any work they are doing and to leave. On no account are they to be molested."

Will and the others on picket duty could usually spot a blackleg a mile off. Their dress and appearance gave them away as not regular labourers.

Another part of the pickets' strategy was to intercept blacklegs before they even got near the docks. Usually they were shipped in on trains from outside the area. Journeys to Silvertown started at Fenchurch Street Station. So Will made sure there were always pickets around the entrances. Once it became known that pickets were ready to receive them, many blacklegs got nervous and never got on the train.

A reception committee was ready there at Silvertown Station. One day, as a train neared the end of its journey, one man with a gun leant out of his carriage window. He threatened to shoot any picket who interfered with him. Fortunately the other passengers in the carriage quickly overpowered him. He was restrained until the police came to take him into custody. Later the newspaper reported that five chambers of the revolver were found to be loaded.

Blacklegs were becoming increasingly unpopular. The strikers regularly abused them with calls such as, "Taking our jobs, you ought to be ashamed of yourselves!" and "Cowards, thieves, go back where you come from." As the strike continued into September, as the strikers' hunger and desperation got worse, so did their anger turn into blind hate. Will was caught up in this mood as much as the rest.

Picketing around the dock gates was a much quieter experience. Will reckoned the weirdest thing about patrolling at night was the eerie quiet and the stillness of everything, instead of the normal bustle and noise due to the constant back and forth of transport vehicles and hundreds of people.

Standing around for hours, especially at night, would have been dispiriting without the company of other strikers. The police were always present, keeping their distance but near enough to be visible at all times. Relations between the two sides could be said to be amicable but guarded. Some days it pelted down with rain and everyone got soaked. Only one thing remained the same – it was the mist which hung heavily over the area.

Will noticed one other great difference – the men were all saying things to each other which had never happened before the strike. It no longer mattered what your job was and however much you felt in competition with the next man before the strike.

"We're all in this together."

"Even if the dockers had to return to work at the old rates of pay, the strike would still be the best thing that ever happened to us."

"We now know how strong we are when we act together."

If Will was not picketing or marching, he walked the streets carrying a collection box. Collection boxes were essential to keep funds coming in to support the dispute. In spite of the fact there were perhaps hundreds of strikers out every day, everybody was proud of the fact that not a single box was ever mislaid.

As week followed week without a settlement, desperate people could be seen wandering the streets everywhere including Charlotte Street. Will knew some of his neighbours had to pawn everything, including clothes and shoes. Others managed to get items 'on tick,' others borrowed cash from friends and relatives.

For most of the street rents went unpaid with no prospect of repayment. In spite of this the wives of those on strike were unstinting in their support, though they knew that their own children were starving.

With the only prospect in the future being homelessness, the workhouse and the break-up of families, for some it all became too much. A couple of households decided to do a 'moonlight flit.' They crept out of their houses in the middle of the night to escape. It was the sound of pram wheels on the quiet pavements at night that gave them away.

Will knew he was luckier than many as Mary's money paid the rent. With little cargo being unloaded, his son Frank had lost his job and was now, somewhat reluctantly, on strike. But they would be able to look after themselves.

In one way the strikers were more fortunate than their families. At least after a long day without any food and just an occasional tea to keep warm, they could find somewhere to go for refreshment. All they had to do was drag their exhausted bodies to the Wade's Arms in Poplar. Here hundreds and maybe thousands, would wait patiently every day for tickets which would be redeemed for food. The landlady was a Mrs Hickey.* Assisted by her son and daughters, she redeemed the tickets inside for cups of soup and some stew. The family kept up this routine throughout the day for each day of the strike.

The distribution of strike pay was another daily event. Outside Ashley House, in Canning Town, a table was set up. Sometimes Will would sit down at the table where the money was given out. At other times he would act as a scrutineer, looking carefully at those who applied. The strikers formed themselves into a queue in single file in the hope of receiving up to one shilling and sixpence a day.

The routine became familiar. "Only those with their union cards can apply," called out one of the scrutineers, a point already known to everybody. But it served as a warning to anyone not on actual strike.

"First to come forward must be those who have claimed less before," called Joseph, who organised the queue. "Let every man get his share before anyone gets two. And if you're trying to claim for the third, fourth or fifth time, you can try your luck later," a polite way of saying 'get lost.'

Another committee man, Tom, who was giving out the cash, would often attempt to be cheery and keep the men's spirits up. "I hope you men won't put any of this money into the bank." This remark always made Will smile. Everybody knew none of them had ever entered a bank in his life.

If there was to be doubt about a man or if someone appeared an imposter, he was spoken to quietly by a scrutineer. They were trying to spot anyone who might have been sent to spy on proceedings on behalf of an employer or who just might be a trouble-maker. If your face didn't fit or there were doubts about someone, such as wearing fancy clothes, he would be told something like, "I'd recommend you get out as soon as possible." If this happened, the man would be allowed to move away unhindered.

Anyone starting to argue in front of the table was quickly grabbed by his shoulders and pushed into the crowd. Once the end of the line was reached, the distribution was over. It generally took three hours each day.

Regular meetings were held outside the docks where the strikers got the chance to listen to their leaders. It was the best way to tell the men the latest news and to encourage them to hold fast. Will was there when John Burns spoke to the men in Tidal Basin. Waving his straw hat about excitedly, he stood on a chair and said:

"I wish to announce that one thousand five hundred pounds has been received from working groups in Australia." Huge cheers went up.

"When the strike began, it was said that in a few days you would be starved into submission. Now more than three weeks have elapsed and we are in a stronger position than ever.

"When you labourers have got what you want, then you must set to work to educate yourselves, not spend so many pennies on bad habits or on beer but work to make your homes brighter and cleaner and strive to make a great improvement in your lives as individuals.

"In conclusion, I want you to promise me that you will continue the strike and never rest until victory is won for the dockers of London and for the women and children of the East End."

This kind of talk inspired Will. It was a view of a better future that he could aspire to.

As the strike dragged on, the press became more hostile. It said the strike committee wasn't allowing the men to decide for themselves on the concessions being made by the employers and it was the pickets who were preventing men from working.

"It was reported that one worker said that more men would be working in Victoria Dock but terrorism prevented them from going to work."

On the other hand, the squeeze on the employers was getting tighter. A decisive blow was delivered by the Watermen's Company. It issued a warning that no barge or similar vessel was to be used by anyone not a member of their liveried society. This pronouncement virtually sealed off many of the boats on the river waiting to discharge their cargoes. None could get in or out.

On the 10th September, there was talk of negotiations between the union leaders and the directors and that the Bishop of London and Cardinal Manning* were urging a just settlement. Then the news got out that Cardinal Manning had come in person to meet with the strike committee in a catholic school near the Wake Arms in Poplar. A large crowd assembled. Will went along and there met Pat and Sean Brady who he'd seen occasionally on picket duty during the past four weeks.

"I think we're going to win," said Pat. "The Cardinal will be putting the kind of pressure on the bosses I doubt they'll be able to resist."

Just then, it happened. The Cardinal himself came into view. With the meeting over, he came out to talk to the crowd. He moved amongst the people with such grace and ease, smiling and stopping to talk with some of the lucky ones. He blessed their struggle for justice and showed sympathy whilst listening to their sufferings.

He gave off such an air of tranquillity that many were close to tears. Cries of "God bless you, Father" and "Pray for us, Father," rang out. Sean turned to Will and said, "I don't know what your religion is, Will, but I'm telling you, this is truly a man of God." Will found it impossible to disagree with him. By his presence, the Cardinal lifted their spirits and made the people feel both worthy and proud of what they were doing. All felt that with the Cardinal on their side, they could believe they were going to win.

Then came the day, Saturday 14th September, late in the evening when, after protracted talks, it was announced that the strike had achieved a total victory – the award of sixpence an hour ordinary time, eight pence an hour overtime. There was to be a minimum payment of two shillings per day and no victimisation of the strikers. Most significant of all was the decision to move the dockers from contract working to piecework.

On Sunday 15th September, there was a victory rally. Will joined the thousands cheering and laughing, with the bands playing joyful tunes. People were dancing and singing all the way from Hyde Park, where the parade started, right across London as far as the Commercial Road. Will, like all those present, felt both exhausted and exhilarated in equal measure.

By the Monday when the docks re-opened, a different mood was upon many men. It was time to get the blacklegs. It was known that a number of them were still working in the Albert Docks. On the Tuesday, a crowd of over a hundred men including Will went looking for them. They spotted about fifty blacklegs and rushed at them. Frightened, these men fled in all directions. Many headed for the Great Eastern railway line.

Twenty odd men found themselves being chased down the track by a crowd of a similar number. Will and his mates, perhaps being stronger and fitter, caught up with those fleeing. Punches began to be thrown. The fighting became vicious. The oncoming presence of a train did not deter the struggle. It took sudden braking by the engine driver to prevent many from being run over.

The footplate-man got down off his train, made for Will and shouted, "Let go, Will! What are you doing? Are you mad? Stop fighting you two." He pulled Will and the blackleg apart. It was Frederick Horth.

"This isn't like you, Will. Come away quickly, before you get yourself arrested." Will did not resist and allowed himself to be taken round the back of the train for safety. The dock police soon arrived in large numbers. They escorted the blacklegs away for their own protection while the Metropolitan Police instructed the union men to disperse or face arrest for trespassing and disorderly conduct.

Frederick was looking into Will's eyes. "Where did you get that kind of anger and hate inside you, Will? Just go home and calm yourself down." Frederick had his arm round Will. It was reassuring. Will felt relieved his friend had not given up on him, like he had done on Frederick.

CHAPTER 13

Drunk on Politics

Will had difficulty calming down. Whilst being happy the workers had won, he was disturbed by his behaviour in fighting the blackleg. As Frederick had said, he had been out of control, stupid as well as endangering the lives of others and himself.

Next day, out of habit, he drifted back to the Wade's Arms. The unions were tidying up, prior to clearing out. Will asked if there was anything he could do to help.

One official replied, "We got some money left in the strike funds. If you like, you could go round the streets giving out cash to those you reckon need it most."

Will agreed and set off down Poplar High Street with ten shillings and five pence. Looking around him, those in need could include anybody. He came across an elderly woman.

"Do you know anyone who's really desperate for a little cash, especially after the strike?"

She looked at Will. "Why, how much have you got to

hand out? There's a few of us need a lot of help at the moment. Though, to be honest, if I think about anybody who's really down on their luck, it would be Betty Skinner. She lost her husband during the strike and can't afford to bury him. He was a blackleg and so people don't want to help, but that's hardly her fault, is it?"

Will asked her for directions. Before leaving the old woman, he gave her a few pennies. He was feeling generous. Off he went to find this Betty, but as he approached the front door, he stopped and thought for a moment. Only two days ago he would have killed a blackleg, now he was about to help a blackleg's family. Was forgiveness starting to enter his head as a result of Frederick's compassionate attitude to all suffering, whatever the reason? Did this Betty deserve help? He had to find out. He knocked at the door which was opened slowly. A face peered nervously out. What it revealed was a person who was overwhelmed by both fear and grieving.

"Betty, can I have a word with you? I'm from the union but I'm here to help you, if I can." Perhaps Will shouldn't have mentioned the word 'union' but next thing he witnessed was this woman bursting into tears.

"I know it's all my fault. Have you come to torment me? Leave me alone. Go away."

"Betty, I understand you've just lost your husband and you need a little help with the costs of the funeral. Look, I know he was a blackleg. But we've all got to get past that kind of hatred. The union has instructed me to offer assistance for those most in need."

Nothing Will said could stop Betty crying. "Let me come in please and we'll see what we can do."

Betty opened the door wide enough to let Will enter the front parlour. In the middle of the room, there was a simple wooden coffin, kept off the floor by two wooden chairs. The room was stripped of any other furniture. The smell of putrefaction was nauseating.

"How long has the coffin been laid out like this?" asked Will.

"Several days now. I don't want him thrown in a pauper's grave but I can't afford to pay for my old man's burial."

"How did he die?" asked Will.

Betty could hold back her grief no longer. "He had wanted to come out on strike but I, may God forgive me, persuaded him not to do so. It was last Friday, on the last day of the strike, as he left the house, he said he had a bad feeling that he didn't expect to be alive when the strike was over. Well, I know accidents happen all the time in the docks but most of the blokes brought in during the strike weren't as careful as the regulars. It was while unloading a ship, a load slipped and tipped my husband into the hold. A bloke came to tell me the news. When I got to see him, his head and body were all smashed up. I had a hard job recognising him until I noticed the brass ring on his finger. We could never afford anything better.

"All our lives, me and the kids have struggled with the bills. But it's going to be worse now he's gone. I'm so unhappy. And he never gave me a cross word. Now I feel I've killed him and I'm not sure I'll ever be able to forgive myself."

"How much does the funeral company want to bury him?" asked Will.

"They said they'd do it quickly for three and six."

Will gave her the money and quietly walked away. As he kept walking eastwards, he came across many children without shoes on their feet, old men shuffling about in threadbare clothing and women with what looked like empty baskets, eyes shifting everywhere for what they could garner in the way of half-rotten produce from the fruit and vegetable stalls. He sensed the desperation, the level of sacrifice and the widespread hardship. In some respects the strike hadn't changed anything, perhaps even made things worse. Had it all been worth it?

Will decided it had been. The way ahead would be long and hard but he for one would continue to fight for a better future for all. There could be no going back to things as they were. The challenge for him was to keep his temper and not become violent.

In a haphazard way, Will moved about, giving out coins – pennies, three-pence pieces and sixpences to those he hoped would spend them sensibly. He could think of no better way of giving away the money and once it was gone, he could do no more.

The next day he knew he had to return to work. He did so without any enthusiasm. He entered the yard and went up to his old foreman, whose face when he turned to Will, bore a look of both anxiety and anger.

"Right load of chaos we have here," he said. "Nobody is sure when we'll get our stock up and running again. Could be days before the docks are back to normal. Let's hope our old customers still want us and haven't gone off and got their coal elsewhere."

"That's unlikely," said Will, "nothing's got in either by rail or sea the past month."

"That's as may be," said the foreman. "Well, Will, you've still got your job for the moment but I'm putting you with a new mate, Mike Thomas. Joe Badman told me he was reckoning on moving to Silvertown so it makes sense to give him a round that way rather than Tidal Basin."

"Joe's moving doesn't stop us working together as before. What's the problem?" asked Will.

"I'm telling you I'm putting you with Mike Thomas. He's a lot younger than you and can help you out a bit. Go and find him and get acquainted. He's down by the stables, looking after your horses. They need a bit of looking after and exercise, having been idle for weeks. Luckily one or two of the men on strike came in regularly to feed and brush 'em down. Appreciated that I did, not like most of you union men."

Mike was friendly enough, though Will was sure he hadn't seen him during the strike.

"Do you come from round here?" Will asked.

"No," replied Mike, "I've just arrived from Billericay, Essex."

Together they loaded up the cart and set off. They

maintained a quiet silence. Will's mind was spinning with doubts as to whether all those who took part in the strike had got their jobs back or had drifted away, like Sean and Pat had done. There was tension in the air. He sensed things were not going to be easy. It also struck him just how much he hated his job. Will had to hope that while he still had a strong back, the company would continue to employ him, but somehow he wasn't bothered.

It was time for Will to get back in touch with Frederick. It took a few days before they ran into each other at the pub. Will went up to his old friend. "It's good to see you again, Frederick. I want to thank you, mate, for what you did that day on the railway line. You're a good friend and I'm sorry I was rude to you during the strike."

Frederick graciously brushed that aside. They shook hands and Frederick offered to buy Will a pint, just like old times. They sat down together but Will noticed Frederick was very subdued. He felt Frederick had something he was holding back. He wondered if he had news of his daughter Emma. "Well, has Emma come back home now?" Will asked.

"Not only did she not come home, she's got herself into trouble," Frederick replied. Then he let out a deep sigh. "Obviously you have not read the 'Stratford Express' lately. In one of those regular reports about the local assize courts, the paper spoke of a match girl from Bow who was sentenced to 14 days hard labour for stealing a shawl. The paper gave her name – Emma Horth."

"That's terrible," said Will. "How's Jane taken the news?"

"She was as devastated as I was. Our lovely daughter a criminal! And we don't know how to contact her. We know she's done wrong, but we still love her and we want to know how she is. I shall have no peace of mind till I know she's alright."

"I have to say I'm sorry for you both but she's a tough nut," said Will, "somehow, she'll get by, I know it. One day she'll come home, I'm sure."

Not knowing when Mary would be around, Will spent his evenings out at meetings organised by the S.D.F. The union leaders wanted to keep up the momentum for political change in the docks. Fiery speakers regularly exhorted their audience to continue the struggle for socialism.

"Socialism," one said, "is the way forward. It is time for the working man to take control. You may work as a docker, or a ship builder or in a warehouse, but first and foremost you must think and act as a socialist."

Another said, "Lots of you men are without work. You probably ask yourselves, is it my fault? Is there something wrong with me? How am I going to feed my family? Well, the first thing to say is that it's not the fault of the working man that you're without a job. You didn't cause the current trade depression – the capitalist system is responsible. It needs knocking off its perch. Give power back to the people I say."

Another spoke of the local council. "West Ham is now a borough. We've got two MPs, and new powers given to local authorities mean that they can tackle problems like the disgusting state of our water and sewage systems. But first we've got to throw out the old rulers. The current council is full of posh people who come from outside the docks. They think they have the right to rule. Throw them out, I say. Put our own men in charge and we can get rid of the filth in the Thames and the spread of infectious diseases."

The times seemed right for change. In 1892 a general election was called. It was the first election in which all male ratepayers had the chance to vote. To oppose the Conservative candidate, a combination of Liberals and trade unionists selected as their candidate, Keir Hardie.★ By now Will was a card-carrying member of the SDF. All their members were urged to spend as much time as possible attending meetings and putting up posters.

It was exhausting work but it paid off. Keir Hardie won the docklands seat of West Ham South. This victory was followed by local elections in which several Socialist-named candidates won office. To Will, these were intoxicating days.

This spirit of euphoria only lasted a short while before Will was given the sack. That day, the foreman stopped Will before he even got to the cart.

"Will, you've been getting a bit wayward in your hours. Mike loads up your cart, waiting for you in the mornings. You're not delivering as much and Mike's complaining he's losing money working with you. You're not pulling your weight, Will. Times are hard enough what with less orders coming in due to less trade in the docks, so I can't afford to have a slacker on the team. Sorry, mate, but that's how it is. Collect any wages due and then please leave." Without saying a word, Will shrugged his shoulders and did as instructed.

As he left the yard where he had worked for many years, he was saying to himself, "What do I care? I think I'm glad not to be doing that job any more. Now I can spend my time doing…" then he stopped. "Doing what? Working for socialism?" That didn't seem a proper answer.

A huge gap in his life suddenly opened up before him. He couldn't deny it any more – he was feeling desperately lonely. Take work and politics out of his life and there was nothing left. Mary was rarely at home. Frederick was busy with his family. Then there was Frank. He had done well getting a job at Tate's sugar refinery in Silvertown. He was busy enjoying his independence, though he still lived at home. He helped with the rent and bills.

What about money? A quick and easy solution came to Will. "I don't need the upstairs rooms any more now that Joe's gone. I'll let it out."

It wasn't difficult to find someone. Within days Will had given the room to a single bloke who had got himself a job as a skilled carpenter in a furniture manufacturer's. "Skilled men are still needed," thought Will.

As time went by, Will began drinking more heavily. To his shame, Will found himself using some of the rent money for drinking. He was constantly tense and excitable, living off nervous energy. He was wearing himself out and not eating properly.

In the 1894 general election, Keir Hardie lost his seat. His time as an M.P. had been controversial. His fate was sealed on the day that Parliament had passed a motion congratulating the Duchess of York on the birth of a son. At the same moment the House knew, but ignored, news of a mining disaster in Wales in which two hundred and fifty men and boys died. In an emotional speech Hardie denounced the royal family. He would not be forgiven for that outburst.

Will was downcast. Deep down inside his glass of beer, he found himself condemning his class – the working class – for being deluded. "Why don't they understand what is going on and think differently?" He was sitting there, by himself, his mind becoming more obsessed with depressed thoughts. That was until an excess of alcohol made him feel more light-headed. He could briefly laugh at himself until his mood returned to one of self-loathing. He knew he was losing control of himself. He was fast on his way to becoming a drunkard, just like his father. At the same time, this resemblance to the behaviour of his father appalled him.

A note was delivered to Will's door one day by his brother Charlie, announcing that their mother had died. Feelings of remorse swelled up inside Will. He had neglected her and the rest of his family. He felt he had let both his parents down and he was becoming as big a disgrace as his dad had been. He remembered his dad's last days when he had looked pathetic. Was he now any better?

He went to the funeral but only stayed as long as he had to. He felt he had left his brothers and sisters way behind in another life. He needed a drink. Later that day he staggered back home from the burial service. No one was there. Hanging up behind the bedroom door was Mary's nurse's uniform, with its mauve striped dress. It was her summer outfit. He looked at it and touched its hem. Mary has done well, he thought, being now a properly trained and qualified staff nurse in a big, modern hospital like The London Hospital.

What had he achieved in comparison? He was always a labourer and would remain one. He had no work and few prospects of getting a job. And he was getting older. He was more educated now than when he started out, due to his own efforts, but what good had that done him? He'd done his bit in fighting for the rights of the working man over the past few years, but was it worth it? At this moment Frank came in from work. He had to sober up a little and be nice to his son.

"Hello, son," Will said. Frank nodded and said hello.

"How's the job?" Will asked. "Where have they got you working?"

"Where do you think?" replied Frank. "In possibly the worst section, among the animal bone charcoal – shovelling the stuff onto the filtering beds, to purify the sugar. It's so hot and stuffy down among the ovens. Still, can't complain. In our gang we all share the jobs around. Somebody has to do the lousy jobs."

"What about the bosses – how do they treat you?" Will asked.

"Our foreman's ok. It must be a good firm to work for, you know. Every day there are queues of men outside the gates hoping to get a job there. The pay's regular, so are the hours," offered Frank.

"The reason why there's men queuing for work is because so many are out of work," replied Will fiercely. "There's a recession going on and thousands are being thrown out of their jobs. The docks, manufacturing companies and the warehouses – they're all losing trade. The moment the business contracts, it's the first reaction of the bosses – get rid of the workers. Their problems then become our hardships and poverty. Augh! I've seen it all before. The system is rotten. You don't understand."

"Dad, I hate you going on about how working men have to get together to take on the bosses, to take over the factories and the railways and to introduce socialism. And what good has all that talk done for you?"

"Frank, I deserved that. And I know I'm not acting like a good father at the moment. I get angry, just like you. But I still believe there is no alternative than to fight for what you believe is right and never get beat. It's an old family tradition of the Waltons. It goes right back to my great grandfather and my uncle John."

"Dad, some of what you say is fine but I think it's down to the individual to better himself. I'm with the bosses. I don't want to knock them down. They gave me a job with regular hours so I can use my own free time to educate myself better – just like you said you did."

"What do you think would happen if the supplies of sugar dried up for some reason? I don't know – maybe the shipments of sugar from the Caribbean stop because of a hurricane – what would take place next? Why they'd get rid of people pretty sharpish. Now if the workers owned the plant, they would safeguard the jobs and find their own solutions to any problem."

"Dad, you can't run a country that way – we'd all be the poorer. And the workers couldn't run a business. I know a lot about shovelling but that's no good for managing finance or designing complicated machinery. You need accountants, engineers, and people like that. Let me be free to try and do what I can for myself. Your union men are just like sheep, waiting for someone to tell them what to do."

"So you don't see yourself as part of the working class? Looking out for yourself and leaving the rest behind, is that what you want Frank?" asked Will.

"Yes," said Frank, "It is. I'll be a rebel my way by standing up for my right to advance myself beyond my class as you call it if that enables me to educate myself and get a good job, perhaps one day becoming a teacher."

"Alright, Frank. Let's leave it there. I'm going out," said Will.

He knew he'd lost the argument with his son. Will wanted to cheer himself up. "My own son, thinking like that," he kept saying to himself. Will felt depressed, and like the weak man he knew he could be, he wanted to go somewhere where he could have a drink to make himself feel better.

He went to a place with good memories, the Hallsville Tavern. Out of pure habit, he ordered a pint of bitter. He didn't need or really want it, but he was having a pint because that's what he always did. He didn't immediately recognise anybody there, which made him feel more relaxed. However someone had seen him. He became aware of a man waving his hand above his head, signalling for him to come over. It was his old friend Frederick Horth. It suddenly struck Will that they had not spoken to each other for a long time.

As he walked over, Frederick said cheerfully, "Hello Will, how are you?"

"Not bad," was Will's nothing answer. Then there was a pause.

"You don't look very happy, Will – what's the matter?"

"Aw, nothing really." Will's reply was so evasive he immediately thought of his father's old habit of never answering a straight question with a straight answer.

"It's alright, Will. I know what's going on. We've all been concerned about you."

"Very kind of you all, but I've got to sort myself out. I know that."

"You know, of course, that booze won't help."

"Well, it'll have to do for the moment. I'm going to get another pint – you want one?"

"OK," said Frederick, "for old time's sake."

Whilst waiting to be served, Will thought hard about Frederick. He felt guilty about how much he had neglected his oldest friend. They had once been so close. Now there was himself, like a smouldering volcano waiting to explode, while Frederick remained cheerful and uncomplaining.

"Here's to you, Frederick," Will said, "enjoy it."

"You seem more cheerful suddenly, Will."

"Perhaps, it's seeing you again, my old friend. How are you and your family?"

"Well, you know me, Will. Not a lot upsets me. The family's doing well. There's only the one thing that gets me down. Do you know what that is?"

"After all this time, it can't be your eldest daughter, Emma. She's not still missing or not been in contact, has she?"

Frederick nodded and a sad expression came over him.

"Is there no news of her whereabouts?" Will asked. "She must have been gone several years by now."

Frederick shuffled again, looking for something. Reaching inside his jacket, he took out an old envelope. From inside the envelope, he took out a piece of note paper and said:

"I've not shown you this before. It's a letter dated July 1892. No address but the postmark says Poplar. When I first opened it, I knew it was from Emma. In it she says that she's met a man with whom she believes she's in love. She's living in the Old Ford area, in lodgings, while she and her fella, Alfred, decide where to go next.

"She admits she's gone off the rails a bit and feels a little ashamed of some of the things she's done but hopes her life will become more settled now she's got Alfred. She says she's thinking about us all and we should not worry about her. Here, have a look for yourself."

Frederick handed Will the letter. "And that," sighed Frederick, "is the only time I have heard directly from her. Silly girl – saying we should not worry about her. That's the very thing her mother and I can't stop doing.

"Then recently I read in the paper about a woman called Emma Haig who was up before the courts in Ilford. She had attempted to hang herself. She was under the influence of laudanum at the time. Her husband had prevented her from killing herself. But the court was also told that she had previously been charged with attempting to throw herself over Poplar Iron Bridge into the river. The paper didn't say whether she was on drugs or not. Anyway, the judge decided to give the woman a severe caution and placed her back into the care of her husband, Alfred Haig.

"Now I don't know whether this woman is my daughter or not. But it scared me and made me wonder if my Emma is in similar trouble. Suppose it was her. As

I say, I don't know and I've heard or read nothing since."

"Have you ever asked the police to help find her?" Will asked.

"Naw, they're not interested. Said they'd got enough on their plate without searching for someone who could be anywhere by now."

"I suppose that's true, what they said. But it's not much comfort for you, is it?"

"I just want to know if she's alright. I don't want to die without knowing that."

For the next few months, nothing much happened. Will sobered up a bit and spent less time in union meetings or reading 'the kind of books clever people read' as one union colleague put it. Then one morning came shocking news, via a note written by Mary and delivered by a hospital errand boy. It read:

"Frederick Horth has had a terrible accident. His condition is very poor. On Wilson Ward. Suggest you visit as soon as possible. Mary."

Will, without hesitation, made up his mind to walk to the London Hospital straight away, as fast as he could. A multitude of anxieties filled his brain – was Frederick dying? Would he get there in time? He knew he owed Frederick so much. Frederick was a better man than he. It was he, Will, who should be the one dying, not Frederick with a wife and family to support.

CHAPTER 14

A New Mission

Will rushed to the hospital accident waiting room. Mary saw him and called him over. "Frederick has been run over by one of his own trains in the railway workshop. His spine has been damaged and there has been some haemorrhaging in one of his lungs. His breathing is very laboured. We think he'll probably survive. However, even if he does, he will be severely disabled for the rest of his life."

"Can I go and see him?" asked Will.

"His wife Jane and Walter are with him at present. Sit patiently outside the door till they've gone. But the sister won't let you stay long because he's so weak."

Will did as he was told. Within ten minutes, the two of them came out. Jane was ashen-faced. All Walter could think to say was, "It looks grim to me."

At the bedside, Will continued to wait till Frederick opened his eyes. He was groaning and in considerable pain. In soft, strained tones he said, "It was my fault, not checking the brakes properly. After all these years working under trains and telling others always to take precautions against accidents."

"Don't talk like that about yourself, Frederick," said Will. "Just stay calm and get yourself better. That's all that matters now."

"Hit by the buffers I was and knocked under the train."

"That's enough, Frederick. Stop blaming yourself. It won't help your recovery," insisted Will.

"If I die there's only one thing I regret not knowing. Do you know what it is?"

Will interrupted, "Hang on a minute, Frederick, what's all this talk about dying?"

"I just want to know if she's alright. I don't want to die without knowing that."

"I know you mean your daughter Emma. There's plenty of time yet for Emma to be found and for you to see her again."

"Sometimes I doubt it, Will. If I survive this, I'm going to be pretty much a broken man."

There was another long pause. Then, without really thinking what he was saying, Will said, "Is there anything I can do to help, Frederick?"

Frederick looked hard into Will's face. Then he said quietly, "Will, will you try and find my Emma? As a favour for an old friend, and a dying one, would you go looking? You're the one person who I would trust to do their best to seek her out. It's perhaps asking an awful lot but I don't know who else to turn to."

After a pause, Will said," For friendship's sake, I'll do

it, Frederick. Obviously I don't know how long it will take or where I'm going to look and there's a chance I won't find her. For you, though, I'll have a go."

A smile came over Frederick's face. "You've made me so happy, Will. Just thinking about you going looking for her will cheer me up immensely. It's a sign of hope." He touched Will's hand. "You're too good a man, Will, to let yourself be destroyed by booze. We've all seen too many go to an early grave that way."

"Now, stop worrying about all that. Just concentrate on saving yourself," said Will.

"I knew you were the one man who would help me," said Frederick. "Fate has played me a bad hand but in my hour of need the good Lord has sent you."

"Now, Frederick, you know I don't hold with all that religious stuff," Will said jokingly. "It's we human beings who have to sort ourselves out and help others without the help of any God."

"Maybe so, maybe not. But I believe this is a good deed you're doing. You have a good heart and you're a good friend."

Again, he touched Will's hands. His eyes filled with joy.

The sister asked Will to leave. He walked quietly back home, and more slowly than he had done going the other way. Mary had told him to expect her at home that evening.

When he next saw Mary, Will without hesitation, went up and embraced her.

"It's good to see you Mary. How has your day been at the hospital?" he asked nervously.

"Well, Will, what has got into you? It must be a long time since you actually asked about my work. And to embrace me as well! Really, Will, what's come over you? What's going on?"

All these remarks were delivered in that humorous, good-natured way that made Will smile and appreciate what a great woman she was. "I love you," he said spontaneously.

"Will, what has got into you? I think you're sober, so what a carry-on is this? Oh, and by the way, I love you too, now and again, particularly when you don't drink too much and waste our money."

"Oh, Mary, that's enough," he replied meekly. "I'm glad to be home to see you. But first things first – how is Frederick?"

"Well, he'll live, but for how long we don't know. He's likely to suffer from bronchitis and in a harsh winter, he could easily be blown away by pneumonia. He'll only be able to walk short distances and then with the aid of a stick. Life is also going to be painful for the poor man."

"How has your day been?" asked Will, "Oh I'm sorry, I've already asked you. Perhaps I don't know what to say." He blushed.

"Well, since you ask, not too bad. Being in Accidentals, it's never a dull moment. From the time we opened at 8am till we closed at noon, we've had, let me see, one, two, three men with awful injuries coming from the docks, several kids down with measles, a hysterical woman suffering from blood poisoning, several drunks with head injuries, cases of whooping cough and a fellow who had been attacked with an axe and whose head had been split open. Then there's Frederick. I'm not sure I've remembered them all, but not a bad score for the day, I'd say. But you know I don't want to talk about my work when I get home. This is my time."

"OK, OK, sorry I asked," Will replied, "I'm still a bit unsettled within myself."

"Are you staying home for some food tonight, Will?"

"Yes, I'm not going anywhere tonight. I think I've got a few things to sort out in my head."

"That's the trouble with you men – always living and spending your time in your heads, rather than just getting on with everyday matters, like women have to."

"Please, Mary, listen for a moment. I need to be serious."

"You're always serious, Will. Serious and worrying about things you can't change. But, tell me, what's up?"

"At the moment I'm too tired to think clearly. I have been a bit stupid lately. You know – not being home regularly. Things haven't been right and I do feel I'm letting myself down."

"Will, you're being very hard on yourself. It's been non-stop for you for years, running everywhere at other people's beck and call, canvassing at elections, attending meetings and studying for hours in the library. You've worn yourself out and you got nothing to show for it. It's time to change all that, Will."

"I know, Mary, I know. Frederick Horth has been telling me the same thing, before his accident. That's what I want to talk to you about Mary – Frederick and what's been happening to his daughter Emma – you know the one who went missing some years ago."

"Of course, I remember. Let's sit down with a pot of tea and you can tell me what's happened."

Will told Mary about the conversation with Frederick and his promise to help find his daughter Emma. Mary looked at him and said, "I think it's a good thing you've done offering to help. And, as you say, it will give you something useful to do and a new kind of challenge. I will help you, if I can."

"I'm not sure how you could," said Will. "At the moment I've got to work out how to start. I don't think asking the police for help would do me much good – round here they know me for being involved in demonstrations. Besides, I don't think she's round here. She could be anywhere in London by now or further afield, maybe abroad."

Mary stepped in, "You said that at the time Frederick received a letter from Emma she had been living in Bow. Although it was well over a year ago, it seems to me that we could start there. If she had a criminal record, it would have been hard for her to find work. This man she took up with may have taken her off somewhere. But people don't usually want to go too far from their roots if they can help it. There are exceptions of course – I'm one for a start – but there's not much else to go on where Emma is concerned."

"So, what are you suggesting Mary?"

"Well, it's just an idea and may not be of any use at all. Don't forget I worked at Mile End workhouse. They would keep detailed records of all the people admitted and discharged from their workhouse. Let me see if I can talk to somebody from Mile End who would let me check their books. I bet somebody will still be there who would know me. Let's give it a go! Next time I get a little time off from a shift, I'll go down Globe Town. It's not far from the hospital after all."

A few days later Mary took the time to visit Mile End workhouse. Luckily for her, the porter was still the same as years ago. John Parsons let Mary in through the front door and she told him she had come back to the workhouse to see the matron. Being now a kindly old man, he wanted to know what had happened to Mary during the past ten years or so. He admired Mary's nurse's uniform and was more interested in talking to her than going to find the matron. Fortunately, the master and matron of the workhouse were still the same – Mr and Mrs Fox. Mary told John she needed Mrs Fox's approval and help to look up some old records. Eventually John went and got Mrs Fox. She gave Mary a critical look at her uniform before saying, "Miss Badman,

I understand you'd like to find some information about a relative you've lost touch with. Is that so?"

"Yes," said Mary, knowing she was about to tell a small lie, "a cousin of mine is dying and would like to be able to find his daughter who has fallen on hard times. She was living in the Bow area although she came from Tidal Basin, West Ham. Is it possible we can check some details going back to around 1890 onwards?"

"The master won't approve of you seeing them without my supervision. So you must follow me, if you please."

Mary was taken into a room which she had never entered before. It was obviously the master's office. As she was about to reach up to get hold of the Admissions and Discharge Book, Mrs Fox asked, "What was the name?"

"Emma Horth, though she may have used the surname Haig," replied Mary.

"Oh, her!" exclaimed Mrs Fox, "she was a rum'un. The trouble we had with her. In and out of here she was, causing such a nuisance. But let's see first if it's the person you want."

It took a few minutes to search the big old register. But when they reached 10th October 1890, they came up with this entry under

Admissions:
Name Emma Horth
Age 18 Unmarried

Number 137471
Occupation Match girl
Religious Persuasion   Church of England
By Whose Order Admitted – Sergeant Bryant, Stepney
Green Police.

Mrs Fox and Mary then checked across the page to the
Discharged columns:

Name Emma Haig, nee Horth
Residence 2 weeks, 3 days
Under What Circumstances Discharged – Alfred Haig,
claiming to be her husband, insisted on her release.
By Whose Order (Discharged) – the Master
Observations on Condition at time of Admission/General
Character and Behaviour in Workhouse – For threatening
behaviour and being violent when drunk. During her stay
calmed down a lot – well behaved.

"I'm afraid that's not the end of the story," said Mrs
Fox. "Strange girl though – she had an awful reputation
for smashing windows and throwing objects at people if
she got angry or was crossed. When she was not drinking,
she was a different person. Now, let me guess, let's try
about three months later…Now….yes, here we are. 20th
December 1890."

Name Emma Haig
Age 19 Married

Number 137532

Occupation Umbrella Maker

By Whose Order Admitted – the Master, on police advice, following smashing of windows at entrance of workhouse.

The Discharge columns went like this:

Name Emma Haig

Residence 5 weeks 4 days

Circumstances Discharged – Husband, Alfred Haig, claimed she had gone missing.

By Whose Order – The Master

Observations etc. – Inmate had requested re-admission. When told it was full, caused upheaval. Master made exception.

Then there was a tiny inserted extra entry: 'Husband insisted on payment for damages to workhouse.'

"She was lucky," observed Mrs Fox. "The police could have pressed charges and she could have got hard labour."

"I think she had been in prison once before, so she was lucky," added Mary.

"I recollect she did try and come back a third time some months later," said Mrs Fox. "She was refused but this time there was no violence. She looked worse than she had been, unhappy, almost desperate. Some spark had gone out of her. I have to say that though she was a handful on occasion, she had a lot of charm – used it to get round men, I reckon. Still, you couldn't hate her. I think perhaps she used the workhouse as a kind of refuge.

"Gawd, what's the matter with me, I must be going soft. But I expect by now things have gone from bad to worse. I dunno how her supposed husband put up with her. Somehow she was asking for trouble and probably, by now, she's had it."

Mary then had a thought. "You said, Mrs Fox, this Alfred Haig offered to pay for the damage done to the workhouse. Was there a bill or receipt for the repairs?"

"I expect so," said Mrs Fox.

"Can I see it, please? Only because it might have an address on it. It could help me to try and locate Emma."

"Oh, I'm not sure about that. Bills and receipts are in a special box. My husband would have to do that."

"Is he in today? May I ask his permission?" inquired Mary.

"No, he's out. Can't you come another day?"

Mary then turned on the charm. The gentle art of persuasion lost nothing on her. "My dear Mrs Fox, you have no idea how busy I am as a nurse. And I'll always remember and be most grateful to you. My experience at the workhouse was of great benefit in getting me started in nursing. And this relative of mine – it's Emma's dad who is close to death and there is not much time to find her. Surely Mrs Fox, you could look at the bill for me. Any address could be vital."

Mrs Fox eventually gave way. She reached up for a special box-folder on the top shelf. After carefully examining its contents, she found what she was looking for.

"Yes, the address here is 146 Usher Road, Bow. Ah, this is interesting. The name on the bill is a John Haig."

"John Haig. 146 Usher Road, Bow," Mary repeated as she wrote the information down. "Mrs Fox, you've been a great help. I knew I could rely on you."

CHAPTER 15

To Bow and Beyond

Armed with the information Mary had given him, Will set off the next day to find Emma Horth. He walked towards the River Lea, then kept along its east bank until he reached Old Ford. The route was not unfamiliar. He had used it before as a means of getting a "late drink" in Bow, where the licensing hours were half an hour later than West Ham, closing time being eleven o'clock. He remembered the presence of ex-coppers on the doors, hired by the publican to prevent trouble.

As he walked along, he was thinking to himself what kind of a mission was he on? On the one hand it was obvious – to find Emma – but he also knew his chances were rather slim. So why was he bothering? Was it for Frederick or was it somehow for himself? Was there some kind of selfish motive involved?

He was unemployed. There was a major depression going on and sooner or later he had to find a job. He was unlikely to find one wandering round London. He knew he had been lucky to get by this far and he reckoned he could look after himself. But he also knew he could think like this because Mary, in spite of her absences, was his rock. Yet he should not abuse this love or fall out with his good-hearted son Frank. His family deserved better than he had been offering of late. He needed a little time to sort himself out.

His thoughts drifted back to Frederick. He resolved that he was on this mission because he wanted to help the man who more than anyone else had helped him to get better educated, even if self-taught. Frederick had helped him to try to ask some of the big questions of life, beyond the harshness and everyday struggles everybody experienced. Frederick knew how to keep things simple – "God how I envy him" – he heard himself say out aloud. Then he realised he had used the word God, an amazing expression from his mouth.

On the east side of the Lea at Old Ford were some of the major factories which had gone up in the previous twenty years. What had once been open spaces had been gobbled up by premises such as a rubber factory. Typically, nearby were the workers' houses, laid out in terraces, along with new street names. In Old Ford Road itself, there were many tradesmen's premises, usually for clothing, but some were more specialised, such as patent leather and shoe makers.

The area tried to appear posher than it was. The men wore neck shirts instead of plain collars and they lived in three-storied houses. However as he proceeded down

Parnell Road, there was an obvious decline in the appearance of the houses. Front curtains were torn, and broken windows were held together with cardboard. Peoples' clothing was poorer, their faces leaner, almost dodgy-looking. Prostitutes hung around doorways.

Into Roman Road, and things changed again. Roman Road had long been famous for its market stalls and shops. Trade was lively and you could always get all sorts of fancy items of clothing, some more likely than not having been stolen from the toffs in the smart parts of London ("No questions asked, guv'nor").

Suddenly, on the other side of the street from where he was standing, he saw a bright light in a shop window, standing out against the drabness of a typical winter's day. Moving closer, he saw it was a small Christmas tree, decked out with sugar plums and candles.

Pawnshops were everywhere. Will had always been fascinated by pawnbrokers. It was one place where people of all classes went without distinction. The only difference was that the better-off tended to use a shop outside their residential area whilst the poorest always used a local place. This day being a Monday, things looked busy. It was often the day when women were known to pawn clothes and even personal jewellery, especially if they were desperate, in order to pay the rent.

These women had to rely on their husbands earning enough cash for them to redeem their possessions on Saturday. Then they had to try and prevent their menfolk spending too much on booze on the Saturday and

Sunday. Even if they could redeem their goods one week, there was still a fair chance the whole process would start all over again the week after. It was good business for the owner because he knew he'd get his money back either from the original owner or from selling their wares. In a way, pawnbrokers acted like a bank for the poor since nobody ever had a bank account.

Just off Roman Road, Will managed to find Usher Road. On the corner was a pub with an unusual name, the Rose of Denmark. Will walked down Usher Road until he came to number 146. All the houses looked respectable enough. The Haigs were not poor, he reckoned. He knocked and waited. Suddenly it occurred to him that this would be the first time he would be asking for information and help regarding the whereabouts of Emma. How should he start?

A woman's face appeared as the front door opened.

"Is it possible to speak to Mr Haig, Mr John Haig, please?" Will asked.

"Who are you, mister, and what do you want my husband for?" the woman replied.

"Look, I'm not the police or any kind of official," Will assured her, "I'm just an ordinary bloke who's trying to help a friend of mine find his daughter. And I am hoping your husband can help me. No more, no less."

"What's your name, mister?"

"William Walton. My friend's name is Frederick Horth."

"Horth, that's a name that rings a bell. Are you sure

you're not bringing problems or causing trouble – you and your friend?"

"No, I can assure you. I'd just like the chance to talk to Mr Haig," Will said.

"Well, you can go and find him for yourself. He's up at the Rose on the corner."

"How will I recognise him?" Will asked.

"Ask the barman." And with that she closed the door.

So back up the road he went and entered the 'Rose'. The barman pointed out a bloke about sixty years old, sitting on a bench along a wall, chatting to some other drinkers. Will reluctantly bought himself a pint of beer, aware he was trying to cut down on his consumption of alcohol. He sat down to wait and listen because the group were in the middle of a lively conversation.

"What I'm saying," said one of the men, "is that it was murder. The old girl had her skull cracked open."

"But how do you know it wasn't an accident? She could well have fallen down her stairs and hurt herself. That's what the police seem to think, so I've been told," said another.

"Probably fell over one of the mice or rats she used to have around her house. Seems the place was infested with vermin," said a third companion.

"Look, wasn't she seen beforehand carrying a bag, probably full of money from the rents she'd been collecting on the properties she owned in the area? I think some thief followed her and bumped her off for the money," said the man who had spoken first.

"Just let's stop trying to jump the gun, shall we?" said the second man. "The police are still hoping somebody will come forward to help them with their enquiries."

"I wouldn't bank on the thief offering himself up, if I were you. Nor is anyone round here likely to help them either. That old hag in Old Ford Road was a nasty piece of work and won't be missed, certainly not by her tenants," said the first man.

"Ah, the police will probably find someone to pin the blame on. They usually do." This viewpoint was voiced by the second man Will had heard speak.

"Now, that's enough," John Haig interrupted. "Let me remind you my nephew works as a copper down Limehouse way. If you knew what he has to put up with and how difficult it is to trace a murderer! Unless there's a good scent at the scene of the crime as to who the murderer might have been, it is darn difficult to get the evidence needed to convict."

"O.K, O.K." said one of the men, "So what do you think happened?"

"Well, my opinion for what it's worth is that somebody broke into her house wanting to rob her, then he had to kill her so he wouldn't be caught. The dead make poor witnesses to a crime they say. Probably the murderer knew the woman and thought she deserved it. He was probably poor and she was wealthy. She just hoarded her money and perhaps he had mouths to feed. But that's just speculation."

"So, if she's rich and he's poor, that makes it justifiable, does it?" said the first man.

"Course not. We can't allow people to go round bumping each other off, if they feel like it, can we? No, the law's the law."

That conversation topic seeming to have come to a close with John Haig's pronouncements on the subject, Will stood up and walked over to the group. John Haig looked up at Will and said, "What do you want, mister?"

"Excuse me, Mr Haig, would you mind if I could speak to you alone for a moment?" John Haig got up and they moved down to another bench.

"Thanks. Sorry to intrude, but I'm on some personal business." Will paused for a moment before he started on about who he was and why he wanted to ask if he was in any way related to an Alfred Haig. He mentioned Frederick Horth and his daughter Emma. As soon as he said the name 'Horth', John Haig's expression changed markedly. His face tightened, particularly around the mouth. He had clearly recognised it, just as his wife had done.

He paused for a second or two before saying, "Now, look, Mr whatever your name is, I'm not happy talking about this. Not only do I think it's none of your business, but I'd like to know how you came by my name and address. You don't look like a policeman, not even one of the new plain-clothes type I've heard about. So I resent you coming up to me, asking me about some man's disappearing daughter as though it's something to do with me."

With his hands held up in front of him, Will replied, "Look, Mr Haig, I understand why you feel as you do. All I ask is that you give me a few more moments to explain things further. I'm not doing this as some kind of police investigation or for any reward. I'm simply trying to help a friend, if I can. I'll happily tell you how I come to be here looking for Alfred. Is he your son?"

"My son, what's he to you?" asked John, a little aggressively.

Will paused, took a deep breath and went through the story. He mentioned Emma's letter to her father, her prison sentence, the newspaper story about an attempted suicide in Poplar and her stay at Mile End Workhouse. Finally he recounted the damage done to the workhouse windows and how he, John Haig, had footed the bill.

John took his time replying. "I am not happy that your wife got hold of these details. Again, nothing to do with her. And I resent your intrusion into my family's affairs. Now, bugger off and leave me alone."

"Look, John – if I can call you that – I understand your concerns, I really do. I have no right to ask you for help or to pry into your family's affairs. I'm sorry to offend you. But unless you are able at least to give me some idea as to how I can see Alfred – I assume he's your son – I'm lost. I appreciate that you actually helped him and Emma after the incident at the workhouse. You want to protect your son – fine – but do you think he will help me, if I ask him? Is Emma still with him? Please John, help me and a dying father. I have no wish to plague you

194

further. If you just tell me how I can locate Emma, that's all."

More pauses. Then came the reply. "That Emma was the worst thing that ever happened to my son. Damn nuisance she was – nearly ruined him. Plague on her, I say. Probably killed herself by now, I reckon. Look, mister, you say the newspaper mentioned Poplar. Why don't you go there and ask your questions?"

"But can't you even give me an address or something to work on?" Will pleaded.

"Alright – I'll give you an address where my son and this woman have been living. It's 69 Spey Street. You'll have to find out the rest for yourself," said John.

"That's all you're prepared to tell me?" Will questioned.

"It is. Now I'm going back to my mates."

"Thanks, Mr Haig..John..all the best," Will said as he walked away.

Will left the pub and stood outside wondering what to do next. His thoughts were with this man, John Haig. He was acting as a very protective dad. He had helped out his son, probably very reluctantly. But as far as he was concerned it was good luck and good riddance to Emma Horth. He certainly did not want to help further.

As it was getting dark, he decided to return home and to pursue a search in Poplar the next day. As he walked southwards he came across the Fairfield Road Match Works. He recalled Emma Horth's part in that dispute.

Would he be able to come across her here again as he had that day years before?

Since the strike, stories had continued to come out of the area. There had been reports of street fights involving the women who worked at the factory. No longer fighting their employers, they fought each other. Disputes were settled outside the gates, after factory hours. It was said the women formed a circle. Inside the ring, the sparring parties fought each other like wild cats – punching, kicking, tearing hair and going for what you might call the sensitive areas of a women's body. The police never bothered to intervene. Only a clear 'knock-out' seemed to satisfy the combatants. Next day, of course, they all met up again at work.

From Bow it was back across the Lea and back down to Canning Town.

Next morning Will decided to set off for Poplar by familiar routes. During the dock strike, he'd got to know parts of the area well. So he made his way along East India Dock Road for some distance before he felt the need to ask for any directions that would lead to Spey Street. Uppermost in his mind was the newspaper report which Frederick Horth had shown him. It had referred to Poplar Iron Bridge and the River Lea as the point from which Emma had allegedly tried to commit suicide. So he felt he was getting close.

He arrived at a street called Brunswick Road. A friendly old lady explained, "Head up this road towards the distillery at Four Mills. There's houses on your left and to your right some open space where you should get a view of the Lea. It's somewhere up there, towards the canal, the Limehouse Cut. Good luck, mate."

As he walked up the street. he could smell the distillery before he reached it. He decided to turn left and passed a new-looking school. Just opposite it, there was Spey Street. "That was easy," Will thought. "Maybe now I'll be lucky enough to find Emma."

The houses were terraced, newish and had a tidy, respectable appearance. Having knocked on the door of No.69, a woman opened it and looked at Will with great suspicion. He appeared too much like a working man, a labourer, she calculated, as she looked him up and down. As politely as he could Will asked if he could speak to either Mr or Mrs Alfred Haig.

"Never heard of them," she said, and was about to close the door again.

"I was told by Mr Haig's father that his son lived here with his wife Emma." Will had learnt how to soften his cockney accent if he wanted to sound more posh.

"I don't know any Haigs and I've never heard of any Emma," said the lady hugging her front door.

Will persisted. "I don't like to mention this, but about three years ago this Emma Haig was reported in the press for having attempted suicide and on one occasion she tried to jump off Poplar Iron Bridge."

"Ah, people are always trying to do daft things like that. Silly sods ["she ain't so posh," Will said to himself].

As for the thought of someone trying to kill herself who lived in this house, it gives me the creeps." She paused for a moment.

"Once I heard talk of a woman from round here, maybe called Emma, who tried to commit suicide by hanging herself but she was stopped in time. 'Course I only heard this as gossip. I've been here some years now. So you see I can't help you. All I would say is that a woman like that wouldn't be round here anymore – she'd be down by the docks area by now, probably living off the sailors, if you get my meaning."

"That's a bit harsh, missus. You're more or less saying she's now a prostitute or something. If I were her dad, I'd be a little upset by what you've just said," Will said firmly.

"Ah, well, didn't mean to sound cruel. But there's so many of them down around Blackwall and I'm sure some of them were once brought up proper-like but have gone downhill. It's easily done, if you're desperate. Now, that's enough of my time spent talking to you. It's Saturday and my old man will be getting off work soon and he'll be wanting his tea." She started to close her door.

"O.K. I'll be going. Thanks. Bye." Will had tried to be nice, but it wasn't easy with her. As the door closed, he was thinking, "Why are people always willing to condemn others? Maybe it makes them feel better, to make themselves appear superior to those below them."

CHAPTER 16

A Lucky Escape

Will walked back down the road. For the first time a certain thought had been put into his head. Could Emma have split with her old man and had she fallen on bad times? Had she had to resort to prostitution to survive or to pay for drugs? The idea appalled him, partly out of respect for Frederick, and partly because while he hoped that Emma was alive, he dreaded the thought that if fate had led her down that route, she might be either diseased or dead by now.

He found himself wandering down towards the river and Blackwall. It was already getting darker and things were livening up. He came across something he'd not seen much down his way – a barrel organ, complete with a dancing monkey. There were pubs everywhere with noisy crowds within, laughing and singing. People were constantly on the move, looking furtively from side to side and suspicious of anyone who might be watching them. At one point Will saw a small bunch of men, coming together for a few seconds. Clearly something changed hands – probably money, but maybe other small items too. He reckoned they were either dealing with stolen goods or indulging in a little "off-street" gambling. Don't look too closely he thought to himself, or you could get into trouble.

At least one or two of the pubs had side doors. Men in sea uniforms, possibly officers, could be seen entering them. Perhaps that was where they went for a few minutes pleasure with a prostitute. He persuaded himself it would be safe enough to enter one pub where the women were hanging around doorways, looking for clients.

Later he couldn't remember the name of the pub he'd gone into. All he could recall was that it was in a rough old area, near the docks. He hadn't had much to eat or drink all day. All he wanted was a pint and some bread and cheese and perhaps a little entertainment. Listening to people's voices, they had a familiar ring to him – they were Irish.

In a far corner there was another group of men sitting around tables which had been pushed together. Will looked at the objects in front of each of them and couldn't believe his eyes. He was amazed to see that they were birds in cages, all in a row. Their owners each had in front of them a pint pot.

"What are they doing over there?" Will asked a man standing near him, also on his own.

"Oh, that," he said, "it's a bird singing contest – to see how often the birds open their mouths and chirp."

"How do they decide the winner?" Will asked.

"Supposed to be the bird that chirps the most times in fifteen minutes," the man replied. "I come here regularly – can't resist it, great fun, especially when the arguments start. I think you're in luck. They're going to start a new round, once the bets have been placed."

"But, that's illegal," Will exclaimed.

"Well, it's supposed to be about buying a round of drinks, but, you know, rules round here are flexible, as you might say."

"I hope the cops are equally flexible," Will added.

"Cops round here are not popular. They know best when to stay away or they're likely to get their heads kicked in."

"As bad as that," Will said.

"As bad as that. But quiet, here we go," the man jumped in.

Will reckoned the man at the head of the table was supposed to be the umpire or judge. He had a watch on a chain held in front of himself. He spoke and all listened.

"Now, though each man keeps his own tally, there's to be no cheating. Let's have a clean contest." A few seconds pause. "Go."

The birds seemed to know their cue alright. The chirping started in earnest. The sound of a dozen birds singing away made quite a noise. The owners were making marks on a sheet of paper. Will was transfixed by the scene. It was wonderful free entertainment. And the birds seemed to be thoroughly enjoying each other's company. They weren't squabbling. There were linnets, budgies, finches – so colourful and beautiful they were.

Fifteen minutes seemed to pass quickly. Once the umpire said, "Stop," the owners of the birds were expected to pass him their piece of paper with the score for their bird. It was time to replenish the beer supplies. After two or three minutes counting, came the verdict. "The winner is Tom Wisheart."

Then the arguments began, good-naturedly, Will thought. Someone complained Tom had also won the last round – was he counting correctly? Someone else reckoned his bird had chirped his heart constantly – he could not understand how any bird could have done better. Other voices shouted, "Give over," whilst expecting Tom to buy them all a half a pint each. The bloke Will was standing next to said, "It's a bit early in the evening yet – they've not drunk enough booze to get really stroppy."

Just then he remembered why he was in Blackwall in the first place. The thought that woman in Spey Street had planted in his brain came back to haunt him. Would he find Emma among the prostitutes in the area? Should he ask any of them and see if they knew anything of her? They probably knew everybody round here on the game and many more besides. And they were always on the lookout, he figured. He decided it was worth a try. He finished his drink and walked out of the pub.

As it turned out, approaching a prostitute and trying to start a conversation was not a smart thing to do. You could approach a prostitute but talking to them was out of the question. "What do you want?" or "What you prepared to pay, mister?" were the limits of their conversation. If you didn't want their services, they turned away.

Will walked after one, pleading with her, "Please, do you know a woman called Emma Horth? Help me, please." Instead of replying, she scurried off to join two other women. He went up to all three of them, repeating his request. "Bugger off, mister," was the reply. The more he tried to get them to talk to him, the worse it got. Then a man came up to Will and said in broken English, "You leave girls alone."

"I'm not touching them, just trying to talk to them," said Will. "What's it to you?"

"You leave alone or I'll kill you," said the man.

The penny dropped for Will. The man was the women's ponce. But Will was not inclined to be threatened by anybody.

"Watch it, mate, don't you threaten me," said Will.

The man suddenly pulled out a knife. Still, at six foot tall, Will reckoned he could look after himself. Will gave the man a kick in the balls and punched him. He staggered backwards. The women screamed and ran off. Just as he thought it was over, another man grabbed Will from behind – a strong man.

It wasn't easy getting free. Meanwhile the first man came back, thrusting at Will with his knife. By a big effort, Will broke free and tried to push away the man behind him, but not as hard as he would have liked. Will swung a punch at the man with the knife, who drew back.

Then came the attack from behind. Will felt something enter his flesh, then a sudden pain as a knife was pulled from his side. The wound inflamed Will and he got wilder. The two men were circling round. Something then struck him from behind and he fell to the ground. It was one of the prostitutes who'd come back and had joined in. By now Will was frightened for his life. Just as he thought he was about to be killed, some other men came from nowhere. They wrestled with the attackers. Then they began to beat the hell out of them.

Will watched all this from the pavement's edge. His side was bleeding badly. While his rescuers were sorting out the ponces, he saw two men were keeping watch at either end of the fighting area. A crowd had gathered.

"That's enough. Leave 'em," said a voice Will recognised. It was his old mate from the strike days, Sean.

The attack being over, the ponces were left unconscious on the ground. The men came together. Another familiar face, Patrick, looked closely at Will and said, "Holy shit, it's Will Walton. What're you doing getting into a fight with those heaps of shit, Will?"

"I was stupid, it was my fault," Will said quietly, in some pain.

"Maybe, but when I saw that heap of trash stab you from behind, I thought that's enough. You weren't doing any harm."

"They probably thought Will was a copper or something."

"That's as maybe. But let's get out of here before the real cops come."

As he was being lifted up, Will asked in a faint voice, "Tell me, Pat, what were the two friends of yours doing watching either end of the street? Were they lookouts?"

"We call them 'crows' – it's our way of spotting the cops – they're our real enemies round here, not the ponces."

"No more talking," said Sean, "let's get Will home and patch him up."

Assisted by these old mates, Will was helped along the road. He was taken to a house in the next street. Once inside the door, Sean's wife said, "Mother of God, what's happened?"

She saw the wound. "Set him down on that chair. Off to bed, the rest of you," she said, pointing to several children.

"Look after him, Mairead. He's an old friend of ours."

Mairead lifted up Will's shirt. Some hot water was on a stove. Using old petticoat rags, the wound was bathed with water and carbolic soap. "You're a lucky man, Will," she said, "it looks like the knife missed anything serious." More old clothing was then used to tie a bandage round his middle.

"Will I need a doctor?" Will asked.

"Maybe, maybe not. Let's give it a day or two and then we'll see."

"Are you staying anywhere in the area?" asked Sean.

"No, I still live in Tidal Basin."

"I don't think you're going home tonight. You can stay with us; that's right isn't it, Mairead?"

"To be sure. Any friend of yours is welcome here."

Next morning Will felt better but still groggy. His sleep had been disturbed by thoughts of the attack and the crazy circumstances whereby he came to be in Blackwall anyway. He then began thinking of Mary and what she'd say, as a nurse as well as his wife. He was confused, knowing he'd been dumb in causing the fight and for not realizing that ponces would do anything to 'protect their girls'. He'd been a fool all right.

Being a Sunday, the whole family, including Patrick and his wife Marion, set off early for mass. Will was left alone to work out what to do next. Below the floor he could hear scurrying feet. Mice or perhaps rats he thought. The house was probably pretty near the River Thames. Thinking of rats made him think of being back in Tidal Basin. All the docks were infested with them. Big buggers, they were, always on the lookout for unattended meat. They could demolish a whole cargo of hams in a matter of hours, if given the chance.

When the family came back from mass, a strong-looking liquor was produced – 'poteen' – they called it. "It'll set you right, this will, Will," said Sean. Fine, Will thought, but at ten in the morning! Some of this liquid was also applied to Will's wound. Accompanied by tea and soda bread, they devoured some breakfast.

Will wanted to mention the sounds under the floor.

"T'is the rats alright. The drains round here aren't so good. Got acres of space they have, the run of the land and water wherever the Thames floods our streets," said Pat. Then they all got to talking.

When Will had finished his explanation as to why he was in Poplar, Sean was the first to speak. "So, what you're saying, Will, is that this Emma you're looking for could be dead or alive; she's an ex-con so finding work would be difficult; she's possibly a drunk or a drug addict; she may have a husband or she may not and nobody's seen her for over five years? Is that a fair assessment, now?"

"You haven't given us any kind of description of her yet," added Mairead.

"She was of a fair complexion, blue eyes, quite tall and slim," said Will. "She bounced about, lively as a cricket. She loved fun and dancing and would get people turning their heads. She attracted people. A bit too headstrong I'd say. I think her parents were too serious for her and she wanted adventure."

"Seems like she got plenty of that. She sounds a bit wild to me," commented Mairead.

"That's probably true," Will said.

"Back to the old question, are they still likely to be a couple or not?" asked Marion.

"I don't know," admitted Will, "but maybe not, is my opinion."

"She tried to get away from him several times," added Marion, "as well as trying to kill herself. Something was wrong in that relationship, to my mind, for her to do that."

"It might have been the drugs talking. Maybe she couldn't do without him somehow," said Patrick. There was a pause. Nothing more could be said about that.

Sean then chipped in. "And you don't know for sure if she's sunk into prostitution, though I still think that's more than likely, especially if she's on laudanum or something worse. She'll need money to pay for the habit."

"I'm after thinking that she's not any kind of prostitute working in this area," said Mairead. "We could ask the Sisters of Mercy, who seem to know them all, if they've heard of an English woman called Emma Horth or Haig. They're mainly foreign women round here and they'd be aware of any girl who was from another part of the East End. We'll ask them."

"There'd be few jobs for a woman like that – probably only factory work in some dreadful godforsaken black hole of a backstreet factory," offered Marion.

"Do we think she could have left the area entirely? You know, left the East End of London and gone somewhere, like abroad?" asked Pat.

"My feeling says she's a local girl, an east ender. I think she would have stayed in London. However, if she's with this Alfred Haig, together they might have gone away," offered Mairead.

"I'm sorry, Will, but, all in all, it seems pretty desperate," said Pat.

"I don't want to give up though, at least not yet," Will said.

"We understand, you're not going to give up on a friend," said Sean.

"I don't want to ask the cops for help," Will added.

"Lord, no," said Sean, "Them bastards won't want to lift a hand to help anybody like Emma. They'd say, 'Let's hope she did herself a favour and jumped into the Thames. And good riddance."

"Shall we try other areas?" suggested Pat. "There's the other side of the Thames to think about, as well as this area. There's some pretty bad spots down in Bermondsey – factories like the tannery works, as well as lots of prostitutes, if we still think we have to consider that possibility. Our cousin Eamonn and his Vera would help out. What do yous think?"

"I think it's a good idea. But before we go any further – how's your side, Will? Are you feeling it were best to rest awhile?" asked Sean.

"It's much better, thank you," Will said, "As long as I don't move about too much, or try stretching my arm, I'll cope for a day or so."

"Right, this is what I'm suggesting," said Sean. "Patrick and I will go with you to Billingsgate. Maybe spend a while there, looking around. Then we'll get someone to row us across to Rotherhithe and Bermondsey. We'll try the factories around that area before going on to Jamaica Road."

"Meanwhile, Marion and I can enquire around the

fish market. They use women as gut cleaners," said Mairead. "You have to be desperate to put up with that stinking, messy job."

"And we'll ask the Sisters of Mercy in Poplar whether they can help as well," said Marion.

"We'll be like a proper search party, stretching out across London," joked Sean. "We'll start tomorrow, when you're feeling better, Will."

"But, hang on a minute," Will interrupted. "You'll be giving up the possibility of a day's pay, all of you, just to help me."

"Why not, Will? We'll stick together – always have and always will," said Pat.

"I really appreciate this," Will said quietly and turned away his head, embarrassed by such kindness.

No more words were said. The next day, after some food, the group set off for exploring areas of London Will had never seen before. In fact, it was rare for people like Will from the north side of the Thames to travel to its southern shore.

They got to the tanyards of Bermondsey. Only the most hardened, downtrodden could cope with the heat, dirt and physical effort of flaying the hides and operating the hot dips. "Nobody called Emma Horth known here," was the owner's comment when asked. He was a hard, unblinking, solid man who clearly ruled his yard with a fist of iron.

It was the same at the jam factory where there was largely a female work-force.

There were plenty of prostitutes about. Jamaica Road was crowded with them. After his experience of Poplar, Will was loath to try to talk with them. Then there were those walking the streets aimlessly, maybe with drink or drug problems. Hatless women, some with black eyes and bandages were out on the streets. At one stage they actually saw a man beating up a woman. Will's group presumed it was his wife or something similar. They did not intervene. Soon after, they were shocked to see shoeless children playing on top of waste heaps.

Apart from numerous pubs, there were several derelict-looking tenement blocks, with frequent windows of broken glass. They were not the sort of haunts anyone would want to enter alone. Yet even here there were several prostitutes with their clients going in and out of doorways. It was obvious the blocks were being used as brothels. For the brothel owners the conditions were ideal. If the vestry was about to catch up with them, they could move about within the tenements to escape conviction.

It all seemed so depressing and unforgiving. They knew people would probably survive somehow, because they always did, no matter how bad things were, but it seemed so bleak a place to live. Tidal Basin was no paradise but at least Will felt that there people would rally round and help each other. Here you struggled alone and probably ended up dying alone and uncared for.

They came across an old harridan with a clay pipe sitting on a doorstep. Will approached her. "Do you know of a young woman, aged about thirty, who came from outside this area?" It seemed a daft question but he had to ask her.

"We all came from outside this area. And as for us women – it's a case of being on the game or starve and hope your minder doesn't beat you too bad. If you're looking for someone here, you'd best give up now. She's had it like the rest of us – finished."

By now Will was fully aware of the hopelessness of the task he had undertaken. He couldn't wait to get out of the area. In Borough High Street, Sean and Patrick went to their cousin's. Eamonn could offer little comfort.

"Borough doesn't have so many prostitutes but there's lots more of them in the Elephant and Castle area," he suggested, "but I think it would be a waste of time going there. Go back, over the river. If it's prostitutes you're looking for, in a manner of speaking, the classier ones are over there."

As they headed homewards, they found themselves crossing London Bridge just as it started to snow. The lights on the bridge, accompanied by lights on either shore, conjured up a scene both magical yet intimidating. The City was alive, yet it appeared to have a malignant heart. It was not a comforting feeling, only one that was unreal.

They walked past the Tower of London, another symbol of oppression, to Will's mind. They passed Limehouse Basin. Just then Will sensed that here maybe was another possible place to explore. Tiredness came over him and his side hurt like mad.

Maybe another day, he thought. The group pressed on until they reached Poplar for a night's rest.

CHAPTER 17

Leave Me to My Fate

After arriving back in Tidal Basin, Will decided it might be best to attend the London Hospital to have his wound checked. So, there he was, the day before Christmas, sitting there amongst the seventy or so people waiting to be seen.

Mary was on duty. By now she was experienced enough to organise both staff and patients in her brisk, efficient manner whilst maintaining her good temper. Whilst Will couldn't take his eyes off her, she never even gave him a glance.

The pressure on the staff was intense. By now all London knew there was an accident and emergency service and all London would be treated – no questions asked, except what was the problem. Many were obvious – people with nasty wounds, head injuries or diseased with some malady. Foul smells were apparent as were the cries and sobbing of the unfortunates.

Twice at least whilst Will was there, everything was disrupted by the sudden crashing open of the doors from the street to admit victims of sudden accidents. It seemed there was a gas works not far away and some boiler had exploded. Face burns, burns to the body and other injuries were clear to see. These victims were rushed into an adjoining room for immediate examination by a doctor. Some time after, somebody came in suffering from a highly contagious disease.

Will remembered Mary once telling him that the season of year made a difference to the number of admittances, summer being worse than winter when epidemics were more prevalent. If that happened, the people with minor injuries would have to be ignored because the whole building would be run off its feet coping with the rapid increase in admissions, the need to wash all bedding and clothes and to scrub all surfaces touched by those affected.

Will had arrived early in the hope of being seen. After a couple of hours a nurse came up to him and on being told why he was there, she invited him into a consulting room. A doctor had a look and felt the injured side. The muscle had started to heal. Commenting on the makeshift bandages, he asked who made them. Will told him and added that a special alcoholic substance had also been applied which prevented infection of the wound. That seemed to amuse the medical man.

"I won't ask you where you got it. Getting injured could be seen as an excuse to sample a banned substance." He pronounced Will lucky – the cut had missed puncturing his right lung by less than an inch.

The nurse applied new bandages and he left the unit. He managed a quick glance in Mary's direction. She came over and Will told her quickly why he was at the hospital.

"What? You stupid man! Why are you putting yourself in danger?"

Before Will had a chance to answer, Mary continued, "I'll be off duty for a shift tomorrow, Christmas day, so I can keep an eye on you. Now, on your way, I'm busy."

While Will had been waiting at the hospital he had made up his mind what to do next in his search for Emma. Firstly, he would take a look at Limehouse Basin. There would be plenty of prostitutes there, but somehow he was increasingly sure that if Emma had gone in that direction, it would be a waste of time trying to find her. There were just too many and besides the women relied on being anonymous.

He then considered the other aspect of Emma's possible situation – the taking of drugs, like laudanum. Limehouse was well known for the presence of sailors and other foreign nationalities, including Chinese. There was a rumour that pure opium was available there in notorious opium dens. Mary had told him that those taking laudanum often moved on to smoking opium, which was potentially a killer.

The day after Christmas, he set off again along East India Dock Road, travelling as far as the Limehouse Cut.

The first thing he became aware of was the market area around Salmon Lane with its vegetable and butchers' booths. If you could afford it, the meat here was always said to be the best in the East End.

At the end of Salmon Lane and moving towards West India Dock Road, the housing suddenly looked pretty dilapidated. Roads like Gill Street seemed to consist entirely of tenement blocks, packed tightly together. It looked very intimidating. "A real thieves' den, I'd say," thought Will. Many dingy doorways could well have been entrances to brothels. Men and women could be seen popping in and out regularly. Will came to the conclusion it would be unwise to wander about by himself. He needed help if he was to make progress in finding Emma.

His thoughts went back to John Haig. "He has to know more than he's told me so far. I wonder whether he deliberately sent me off to Spey Street, knowing it to be a dead-end. He just wanted to get shot of me. He's got to know where his son Alfred is."

The next day Will set off again towards Bow. Hoping that John Haig was no longer working all hours of the day, he would try his luck by going straight to the pub, the Rose. Luck was on Will's side, but as soon as John Haig saw Will, the look of disapproval was obvious on his face. He was alone this time. The pub was quiet and Will was determined to get more information if he could whilst remaining polite.

"Hello, John, I know you didn't expect to see me again, but here I am," Will said.

"I can see that. You haven't come to plague me again, have you?" John replied.

"Course not. I want to be friendly. With your help I got to Poplar but I didn't find your son or the woman I'm looking for. So I thought we could try again and see if there was something else you could tell me."

"I don't think you got my point previously, mister. Stop asking me questions about my family and sort your problem out your own way."

"But that's it, John, I can't do it. I need to talk to your son, friendly-like, and then I promise to leave you all alone."

"Has it occurred to you my son may not want to talk to you. Because, if that's the case, you're stuffed, aren't you?"

"Yes, but where's the harm in talking to him? As I said before, I don't want anything off him, just a little help. If he's with this woman Emma still, I shall be more than happy to tell her about her father, then leave. If she's not, is it asking too much for him to try to tell me where he thinks she might be? That's all."

"Mister, you're a pain in the backside."

"Well, that's how I am then. It gets me into trouble I can tell you. But, seriously, let me buy you a beer and let's spend a few minutes talking together. I'm not begging, only asking," Will pleaded.

"I'll have a pint of mild and bitter. Sam, the barman, knows how I like it."

The barman nodded when Will spoke to him. More bitter than mild it seemed John preferred.

"Make it two, please," Will said. Then he went back to John.

"My missus would kill me for telling you this," John began, "Alfred had a rough time with her. They may have been in love, I don't know, but there were some falling-outs as well as good times. It was the laudanum that did it – she couldn't kick the habit, though I believe she tried.

"The worst of it was when she had hallucinations and went a bit mad, threatening to kill herself. Poor Alfred did not know what to do. He couldn't cope – nor could any man, in my opinion. So he gave her up. Where she went to, I don't know. Things have moved on and my son is with a new woman, a sensible woman, and I don't want anything to upset their happiness." He paused before continuing.

"This is what I'll do for you. I'll tell you his address and give you a note to hand to him." With that he went up to the bar and asked for a piece of paper and a pencil. He wrote something on the paper. He then walked outside the pub into the street, coming back two minutes later with a sealed envelope. It had the name 'Alfred' on it.

"My son lives at 45 St Thomas's Road, Finsbury Park. Don't bother going till the evening – he's out at work till about 7pm. When you see him, give him this note. He'll make up his own mind what to do next. Now, that's all I'm prepared to say or do."

"I do appreciate what you're doing, John. Thanks, mate."

"You know, mister, if you weren't such a nuisance, I might even like you. I should wish you good luck, though I'm not sure what for."

This time they shook hands. "He's a good dad to have," Will said to himself.

That same day, in the evening, Will made his way up towards north London. It was a strange feeling, going back Islington way. It had changed so much since the 1860s. Far more built-up, of course, less feeling of being on the edge of the countryside. Far noisier – the sound of horse-trams, carriages, but not so many carts.

He used a tram-car to go up as far as Finsbury Park, an area he had never been to before. The houses and the park looked posh. Many looked new, two or three storied dwellings. They even had small gardens, front and back. Will reckoned they were probably the homes of the sort of people who worked in City offices or who were tradesmen. Probably such accommodation was much sought after. It was also just a residential area – there were no shops or drinking houses. Alfred, Will thought, must be doing well for himself.

He found St Thomas's Street and walked along till he came to No.45. There appeared to be three separate homes – one in the basement, one at ground level and an upper floor. Which was Alfred's? But he needn't have worried – the names of the residents were beside the door pushes. Neither of the upper floors had the name of Alfred Haig, so he went down a couple of steps to the basement and there was the name.

He pressed the doorbell. The door was opened by a young man, aged about twenty-seven. He had a ready smile on his face and a twinkle in his eye. His clothing was that of a working man, except that he was wearing a shirt and collar, trousers and shoes, not boots.

"Hello, can I help you?" he said.

"Mr Alfred Haig?" Will asked. He replied yes. "My name is William Walton. Before I say any more, I have a note for you from your father."

Will offered him the sealed envelope. Alfred tore open the envelope and swiftly read the contents of the note.

"Who's there?" enquired a woman's voice from within.

Alfred pulled himself together. "It's alright, my dear, just a friend of my dad. Shan't be a moment." He pulled the door to, with himself on the outside.

"Now, look here, my dad tells me I should have a word with you but warns me you've come about Emma Horth. He advises me to talk to you if I wish but to keep my wife out of it. I'm just having my meal at present. I want you to make your way to Seven Sisters Road. There's a pub just a hundred yards along, on the left, called The Tollgate. I'll meet you in the public bar in half an hour. Is that alright?" asked Alfred.

"Sure, fine," Will said. With that, Alfred closed the door and Will was left to make his way to the pub.

Will sat in the pub and waited. Sure enough, Alfred came in. He sat down. Will offered him a drink, which he accepted. Once they were settled down, Will told Alfred about himself, about Frederick Horth and why he was hoping to find whether Emma was alive or where she was.

"This isn't easy, my friend. Not for me. And God forbid if Nellie, my wife, found out about my past affair. Are you married, Will?"

"No, my woman works as a nurse." Will replied, "It'd be the end of her career if she was married. I've known her for over twenty years now. Why do you ask?"

"Well," said Alfred, "It's just women seem to come in all shades. There's the quiet ones, dutiful, caring and easy to get on with. And there's the ones who are a real handful, who seem more content to make life difficult for themselves and others by constantly making demands, or who never seem satisfied with anything they're doing. That's the problem kind for any man, I can tell you.

"God, the trouble she, Emma, gave me. The arguments, the fights, the storming-outs, and the not-knowing what she was going to say or do next. Then the next moment, it could be all peace and loving, kind and sweet. I didn't know where I was with her. And she could be so forceful. When she'd decided on something, woe betides you if you got in her way. I didn't know how to handle her. Blimey, I tried. It wore me out. I did my best to please and also to support her when she got

222

down. I tried to protect her from herself. Deep down I think she cared for me and I for her, but in spite of our efforts, things didn't, and perhaps never could have worked." He paused for a moment.

"I don't know why I'm telling you, a complete stranger, all this, but perhaps I've never let go my frustrations before."

"That's alright, Alfred," Will said, "I'm not a bad listener – for a bloke."

"Well," Alfred continued, "the problem was that we didn't see each other for much of the day. I was then working all hours as a porter. Emma was finding work, where she could, no questions asked. Did you know she'd once been done for stealing a shawl?" Will nodded.

"She always said that was an accident, a misunderstanding, but the stall-holder wasn't having none of it. He and the police ran her in and she spent time in Holloway. She said that was possibly her worst time. She felt so ashamed of herself and was scared stiff of her father finding out. That was also the time when we first met. I was young then, messing about with my mates in Bow.

"I was seventeen. I got my first sight of her when she was entertaining in a pub as a singer – she had a lovely voice. She relied on earning odd coppers to feed herself. I made the mistake of buying her a drink. I soon became infatuated with her. I got her some work in one of the back-street clothes factories around Old Ford Road. It made poor quality umbrellas and sun shades which were for export to India and China. Lucky to get even that kind of work really, but then she could talk her way into anything.

"She was starting to get into trouble with the police, being violent and abusive. They thought she was drunk, but now I reckon it was as much about drugs as alcohol. They decided to put her into the workhouse. Against the advice of my father, I went down there and got her out, claiming to be her husband. That happened twice."

"Yes, I know," Will said, "My missus, who worked there once, saw the records at Mile End workhouse."

"Has she?" remarked Alfred, "You have been busy between you."

"And how your dad bailed her out by paying for damage caused to the workhouse windows by Emma," Will added.

"Yes, well, we decided to get away from Bow and went to Poplar. But, you see, it wasn't until we lived together that I got to find out about the laudanum. I don't know when she first took up with laudanum. Maybe that's why she stole the shawl – for cash to buy a supply.

"It amazes me. That stuff is only supposed to be available from a chemist's with a doctor's approval but that's not how it happens. The stories people tell to get hold of it. 'Having problems with my nerves.. can't rest or sleep…need a form of sedation'… that kind of stuff – and you can get it. Bloody dangerous it is. Unpredictable what it can do to you.

"Maybe she was getting too used to it. Or she was

increasing her dose. What I did notice was that she was starting to have what they call hallucinations. She'd go off into a kind of trance and become unaware of what she was doing. Bloody frightening it was. I didn't know whether to be angry with her for not telling me about the problem earlier or angry because of what she was doing to me, let alone herself.

"We began to have furious arguments, which didn't help matters. We started to have money problems. I couldn't be sure whether she was not working or whether she was spending any money we had on laudanum."

"And do you think it possible that taking laudanum had something to do with her trying to commit suicide?" Will asked.

"You know about that too, do you," replied Alfred.

"I heard she tried to jump off Poplar Iron Bridge," Will said.

"Oh, that day!" sighed Alfred. "Fortunately somebody saw her trying to climb up onto the parapet and hauled her back down. The bloke then got the police. A copper came out and rushed to the bridge just in time to stop her a second time. This time they kept her in jail until the court hearing. I assume you know the rest."

"Yes, Will said, "You saved her bacon again. You were a good bloke to her."

"That's as maybe. Or stupid. But I loved her, you see, and by now I kind of felt sorry for her. And that just made her behaviour worse."

After a few more seconds of pausing, Alfred continued. "Anyway, we couldn't stay on in our place in Spey Street. So we had one last go, staying briefly in Hackney. Then she tried to hang herself. That was when I reached my limit. Emma was a contradictory mess. Sometimes she felt guilty, remorseful and depressed and I felt she needed my support. At other times, she resented my help and felt it was not my job. Finally she admitted that she had been unkind, ungrateful, a bad woman who didn't deserve help. She said she deserved her fate. She loved me but had to let me go. There were so many tears, so much unhappiness. It nearly broke my heart. In the end she drove me away. Her final words to me were, 'Leave me to my fate. When I can't get my fix, I become terrible. Don't want to steal to buy more. I don't know what I will do, except kill myself.'"

Alfred couldn't stop now. "I told her she mustn't do that to herself. 'You need help,' I said, 'If not from me, then somebody else'.

"I was desperate myself and unsure what to do. What haunts me to this day were her last words to me: 'If you want to find me again, look for me in Limehouse. That's where I shall destroy myself and bother nobody further'.

"I didn't understand quite what she was on about. All I knew was that she probably meant it. And that's it, Will. I haven't heard or seen Emma these past few years. But I have been able to put it all behind me. I met Nellie. We got on famously. We got married – properly that is – and our first child is on its way. We've been lucky to get this place in St Thomas's Road. And, after training, I have started my job as an electrician, in a new industry with fantastic prospects. I'm a lucky man."

"I'm very happy for you all," Will said, "but just two last things. First, had Emma changed much in appearance from when you first met her, and say up to five years ago?"

"Well, she was still a young woman, comparatively speaking. So if you knew her from the time when she was fifteen or so, then her appearance would appear to be similar. One thing would be different though. On her right lower arm, just above her right hand, there's a burn mark, about three inches long." He indicated on his own body while saying this.

"She said it was a result of an accident using phosphorous from the time when she worked in the match works. Apart from that, I'd say she is the same."

"Secondly," Will continued, "the other thing is to do with Limehouse. I've been there – round the Causeway and West India Dock Road. It all looks pretty grim to an outsider. I'm never going to be able to penetrate that area in safety, by myself."

"I've got the answer for you, Will," said Alfred. "My dad's brother lives in Limehouse – has done all his life. And as luck would have it, this uncle of mine has a son who works at Limehouse police station. I think he's an inspector now. Ask my dad for the address of his brother and ask for an introduction just like he did for you to get hold of me."

"It's very kind of you to make that suggestion," Will replied, "I'll do just that. However, whether your father wants to see me again, I doubt it. I know he thinks I've plagued him enough."

"Oh, he's like that at first with most people." Alfred said. "A bit cautious with strangers and why not? Tell him we've spoken and I'm sure it'll be alright."

"Glad to have met you, Alfred. Good luck with the new trade," Will said.

"Thanks. Nice to have met you too. Good luck with the search. I hope Emma is still alive." These were Alfred's parting words.

So back Will went to Bow for the third time. Poor John Haig didn't know what to make of seeing Will again. But by now he was softer in his attitude towards him. He asked Will about his meeting with Alfred. Having told him how that went, Will mentioned the idea of John giving Will another address – that of John's own brother in Limehouse. He agreed to do this but this time it was Will who wrote out the note, at John's direction. John added that Will should simply tell his brother, whose name was Robert, what he wanted and his brother would contact his son, now Inspector Haig. John and Will shook hands and separated, after one last drink together in the Rose.

CHAPTER 18

Into the Den

Will found the place from the business plate outside a small block of offices in Limehouse Causeway. It announced, 'Robert Haig. Boat Builder since 1870'. Inside the door were two desks, one for a secretary, though nobody sat there that day, and one much larger desk behind which sat this elderly gentleman. Robert Haig looked a lot like his brother, but perhaps a bit thinner as well as being older. He looked the picture of a successful businessman and was smartly dressed.

Will introduced himself and told Robert his brother in Bow had suggested he come and talk to him. "He said you had lived in Limehouse nearly all your life. He said there wasn't much about the place that you or your son didn't know."

"Have you ever been in Limehouse before Mr Walton?" Will said he hadn't.

"In my early days, Limehouse was a place full of all sorts of people, but they were the reliable, honest sort.

Today it's a den of vice and crime. I reckon most of the thieving and the fights round here are started by people from outside Limehouse. Fights between dockworkers often seem to break out because they can't understand each other's language and easily take offence at the smallest thing."

"In my part of the world, West Ham, people are more interested in finding work than starting fights," said Will. "There's not as much work as there was once in Victoria Docks. But, tell me, are the limekilns after which the area got its name still here?" asked Will.

"Yes, they still make bricks. Too many I reckon. They've been building too many houses I'd say."

"The wharves and the local market I passed on the way here looked busy enough," said Will.

"A lot of the ships and small craft here spend much of their time moving and delivering cargo up and down the River Thames," said Robert. "We still land fresh fish. The fruit and vegetables are shipped in from farms up and down the river. From the local slaughter houses, you can get good fresh meat.

"I've always loved the market ever since I was a kid," continued Robert. "My brother and I used to wander around the stalls, seeing if we could do odd jobs for a penny, helping the coster-mongers. Then there were also the fancy stalls selling fancy items of clothing and shoes, all home – made. I can still remember one particular stall which sold 'proper gentleman's trousers.' Another I recall had this sign over his stall which had the name of the proprietor as 'Master Baker Frederick Schnabel'. He was a local character, he was. We'd heard stories saying he originally came from Germany, worked as a sailor, then as a publican before becoming a baker. People rumoured that he was seventy-five years old!

"When we were kids, John and I once asked each other, if we had the chance, which of the jobs we could see around us we would like to do for a living. I said how much I loved the river and wanted to work on anything to do with boats. John said he liked the idea of being a butcher. That way, he said, you might get to eat some of the meat you could not afford to buy. And blow me down, John became a master butcher and I became a boat-builder.

"Anyway, the place has now got too crowded. Law and order has deteriorated and I feel it is no longer safe for my family. So, whilst I've kept the business going down here, we've moved out to Victoria Park to live in comfort and security. Of my family, my son Edward is the only one who wanted to stay and work here."

Robert Haig stopped for a moment. "Must be a sign of getting old. I talk too much about the old days. Now how can I help you, Mr.. sorry I've forgotten your name."

"Please call me Will. I've met your brother John a few times. He suggested I should talk to you and your son since your son might be able to help me," Will said. "I'm looking for a relative [ok, a small lie, he told himself] who may have come to Limehouse in the last few years. She may have got caught up in drugs or one of the opium dens I heard about. Would your son be willing to help me locate her, do you think?"

"Well, he certainly knows all about the crime scene in Limehouse, so why not? He knows all the brothels and these opium dens they have somewhere here. By yourself, you'll get nowhere without police help. It's too dangerous for a stranger, unless he's looking for a whore. Too many foreigners involved in that trade, also the drugs. Disgusting it is." Robert was back on what seemed to be his favourite topic – foreigners.

"So, do you suggest I just walk into Limehouse police station and ask for your son?" Will asked. "I hear he's an inspector now."

"Yes, he's a bright boy. I'm very proud of him. Following in his grandfather's footsteps, he is."

"So, are several of your family or your brother's family in the police?" Will enquired. By now he was getting nervous, thinking of policemen as never having been his best friends.

"No, it's just Edward. Though I believe one of my brother's sons-in-law is a dock constable. But being a copper goes back a long way in my family, back to my dad's time around 1840.

"My father was one of the first policemen on the streets of London. As you are probably aware, for hundreds of years thieves, murderers and other violent people got away with their crimes because there was nobody to stop them. It was a wonder that nobody had done anything about the situation before a man called Sir

Robert Peel★ took hold of matters and established the first proper police service."

At this point Will decided just to sit back and listen and wait to get back to talking about John's son, the inspector.

"Do you know what a stovepipe is?" asked Robert. Will quietly shook his head.

"It was a kind of top hat, dark blue in colour. It had supports inside which made the hat strong enough for a man to stand on and not break it. It was meant to protect officers from blows on the head. My father also had a coat which had leather straps round the collar which was designed to protect them from being strangled from behind. All the officers knew they were taking risks. They used to go round together if necessary to protect each other.

"One day my father was called to a brawl in a pub. Everything was being smashed and men were fighting each other. My father and other officers intervened. In the course of a struggle, my father lost his helmet. That gave somebody the chance – who he was, was never found out, though some suspect it was the dishonest publican who my father thought was watering down his beer. Whether it was him or not, somebody smashed my father over the head from behind with a metal rod. His skull was badly fractured. The men who had been fighting scattered rapidly, leaving the other officers to carry father as quickly as possible to a doctor. Unfortunately, my brave father died within minutes."

There was a poignant pause. Robert still felt the pain at the loss of his father. "I was only six years old at the time. John was just one. It was hard for my mother, bringing us up by herself. She never stopped grieving for my dad, if truth be told. We had to leave the tied accommodation in Cloak Lane in the City and come and live here."

There was another pause before Robert Haig pulled himself together and took notice of the presence of Will and what he had come to see him about.

"What I'm going to do is to send a note to my son straight away. You, I would suggest, should turn up at the station tomorrow. By then, Inspector Haig, as you will call him, will know you're coming and that you want the chance to be taken round the dodgy places in Limehouse. Is that alright?" Robert finished.

"Fine," said Will. "Thanks for talking to me. I can listen for hours to stories from the past though I'm sorry for what happened to your dad. He was obviously a brave man. My own dad told me once how he had lost his mum when he was very young. Leaves a mark when this happens, I know."

"Maybe, but we all cope somehow. Well, good luck in your search."

Will was very nervous about visiting a police station. For years he had avoided them. Whilst he'd never been arrested or convicted of any crime, he couldn't forget hitting a copper and being thumped in return. There was little love lost between the police and the Socialist Democratic Federation. To the police, Will and his like seemed to be threatening social revolution.

He also recalled the days of the docks strike. The police and the pickets barely tolerated each other. The pickets constantly faced masses of police watching their every movement. Law and order to the police meant keeping everything quiet and the same – no rocking the boat. In his most angry and revolutionary moments, Will simply saw the police as there to carry out the wishes of the ruling classes.

Now, here he was, about to walk into a police station of his own accord, asking for their help. He respected the police as brave blokes and there in order to tackle crime but could a cop ever be your friend?

Will walked through the door of Limehouse police station and approached the desk. Having given his name, the duty sergeant duly asked a constable to announce Will's arrival to the inspector. A few minutes later, the inspector came through a side door and introduced himself. He looked a little young to be already an inspector. He was a burly fellow – there'd be no messing with him. He turned to Will and announced:

"I'm prepared to take you round West India Dock Road, as a favour to my dad and uncle. All I want to say to you is that if you find some reason to want to enter any premises, I'll have to go in first. I wouldn't be undertaking this kind of tour in the evening, not without the assistance of other officers. But, in the daylight, I will offer you a couple of hours of my time. Are you ready?"

"Yes, sure, thank you," Will said, slightly hesitantly, "I appreciate you helping me find this relative."

"The more the public understand what we're up against, the better, isn't that right, Sergeant?" He glanced towards the desk. Faced with this question from his superior officer, the sergeant agreed. Then, with a quick nodding all round, the inspector and Will set off.

It wasn't many minutes before they reached Beccles Street. "This here street," Inspector Haig intoned, "used to be called Jamaica Place. The authorities, in their wisdom, changed the name to try and improve its reputation. They're wasting their time in my opinion. It's a hideout of Japs, Chinks, Lascars and other undesirables. The Japs are the worst – always getting pissed. I think they're trying to be like the English." This was the inspector's little joke.

"The people round here, either they're running brothels or they're using them. The owners can set up a brothel and if busted for immoral earnings, simply open up in another flat not far away and start up again. Can't touch the whores themselves unless they molest people or disturb the peace, which happens frequently enough because they get drunk or they're taking drugs.

"The other sort we get are the thieves. These blocks are ideal hiding places. I can't tell you how often my men have been chasing a thief into these streets, only to lose them somewhere, either in Gill Street that way or Rich

Street to our left or West India Dock Road which is not far away down there." All this information was accompanied by the inspector moving his arms about according to the direction he was pointing.

"There's many an alleyway or a courtyard where they can skive in and out of and we haven't got a chance of finding them. If we come into the area in force, we run the risk of having any one of our number attacked, usually from behind. So we prefer a softly, softly approach to avoid putting our officers at risk."

"It's a tough job for you, Inspector," Will commented, "your men must be very courageous."

"Courageous or stupid, sometimes I don't know which," he replied. "Now, tell me who exactly are you looking for? Any information or clues you've got?"

"She's a woman about twenty-one years old," Will replied, "fair and quite tall and English. I don't know whether she's here now or not but I believe it was perhaps three years ago she came here. And, I have to say, she's probably a drug addict."

"What's her name?" asked the Inspector.

"I think she'll still call herself Emma Horth," Will offered.

"Emma Horth. That surname doesn't ring a bell. Emma, you say. But nobody usually uses their right name round here." He paused and took on an even more serious look. He was clearly wondering what he should say next.

"Now, I have to tell you there are a few opium dens

down Beccles Street, in a courtyard called Nightingale Place. Another daft name! There's a place there where an opium den is being run by a woman and a man. He's a coloured man from India, she's English. Why she took up with a coloured man, beats me. The woman seems to run the business."

"Why I can't just bust them, I don't know, but the law doesn't prohibit the use of dangerous drugs that can kill you. Plain barmy if you ask me, and why anybody gets involved is beyond my comprehension. But since they're here, these drug addicts and their suppliers, it makes sense for me to humour them and that way keep an eye on them.

"The woman's name I'm not sure about. I just call her 'Auntie' as a joke. It gains me an entrance, not that the woman is hostile to me at all. So, do you want to go see for yourself? But I warn you, it might be quite a shock to you."

The inspector gave Will a chance to weigh up the option of not going on, but he had little choice. "I've got to try it. That's why I came. Please lead on, Inspector."

So down Beccles Street Will and the inspector went. They soon passed what looked like a doss house. Old men, or those who looked old before their time, wandered about amidst the filth and rubbish all round them. It was like viewing creatures who were already in hell, damned to live out their lives in torment. Then they came to King's Court. They moved quickly. "Haunt of thieves and violent criminals," whispered the inspector.

They were passing tall buildings separated by less than five yards from each other. Dark doorways seemed to contain ghostly looking figures. Even the prostitutes preferred to keep themselves inconspicuous here.

They reached a doorway, marked No.13. Giving Will a quick glance, Inspector Haig knocked on the door, calling out, "It's me, Auntie, may I come in and bring a friend?"

"Come in, my dear, it would be good to see you and your friend is most welcome." It was the sound of a woman's voice but with a harshness about it. It came from an inner room.

Will and Inspector Haig entered a small room before passing through into a large dark room. The greater part of this room was taken up by a large low bed, two sides of which had hanging curtains drawn back. In the centre of the bed was a tray with a small light under a glass bowl. The flame was smokeless due to the use of some special oil. Three or four little bottles were round the lamp. Reclining on either side of the lamp were a man and a woman.

Will was bursting with anticipation. "Hello," she said to him, "how can I help you?" She reached out her right hand to shake Will's. There it was – the burn mark on her arm. "You're Emma," Will exclaimed, "Emma Horth."

CHAPTER 19

Wisdom from an Unexpected Quarter

Emma was the first to recover herself. Putting on a slightly posh accent, she said, "I don't know who you are but you're most welcome here."

"I'm William Wal..." Will started to say before the Inspector interrupted.

"Excuse me, but it would appear, Mr Walton, that you've found the person you were looking for. Now, if you don't mind, I'll be getting back to the station. See you again, Auntie."

"I look forward to seeing you soon, Inspector," said Emma.

"Inspector Haig, thanks for your help. Much appreciated it is," Will said.

"That's alright, sir, all in the line of duty. Always happy when 'missing persons' so to speak, are found by family or friends. So, I bid you goodbye."

As the Inspector passed through the doorway and

then out onto the street, Emma turned to Will and said, "Of course I recognise you. And I have an idea why you're here. But you'll have to excuse me a moment. You may stay if you wish."

With that, she turned to the man lying on the bed, who without hesitation knew what to do next. On a rack at the back of the bed, there were several pipes. He reached up for two of them and gave one to Emma. The pipes seemed to be made of wood, about two-and-a-half feet long. They had a bowl at the end. Emma then picked up one of the small bottles on the tray and a tiny spoon. A thick, treacle-like substance was spooned out and placed in each bowl. Next, the tip of a small knitting needle, which had also been on the tray, was dipped into the bottle before being inserted directly into the flame. When hot, the needle was then held prodded into the bowl of each pipe. This was done several times to kindle the contents of the pipe.

By now, both smokers held their pipes in their mouths. The next move was to hold the needle and the pipe over the heat. Both Emma and the man began to breathe in deeply. This encouraged the bowl to produce smoke. After several puffs, it became possible to blow the smoke out through the nostrils and the mouth. It seemed to take a few minutes for the smoke, which was light blue in colour, to become freely available, enough in fact to fill the room. The smell of the smoke was surprisingly pleasant.

Emma and her partner were lying back on the bed,

with a cushion to prop themselves up. Their faces looked very relaxed and contented.

"You must forgive me, but I needed this smoke. I can't function properly without it. It gets up my courage. I've got to be able to handle what I suspect you're going to say. By the way, there are more pipes in the rack if you feel like joining us."

"No thanks, Emma, I've had troubles enough of my own with alcohol, without trying what you've got there. It's opium, isn't it?"

Emma nodded and said, "And of a very good quality, isn't it, Adi?"

The man nodded, without saying a word. Ever since Will had arrived, he had been observing Will closely while Will was doing the same. To Will he looked a proper gentleman, what with the quality of the clothes he was wearing – an elegant cravat, attached collar with a white shirt, waistcoat and well-fitting patterned trousers. He had a moustache. Even in the darkened room Will could see a white glint in his eyes. He seemed to be smiling gently. Maybe it was the opium but he appeared so relaxed, in spite of Will's feeling that he was completely out of place in this dive of a house, in such a seedy part of London.

"Emma, I'm here because," Will was interrupted by this Adi, who in a quiet voice murmured, "Shh. Don't be in such a hurry. There will be time enough for talking."

Will sat therefore, quietly reflecting on the crazy scene he was now witnessing. It was like a make-believe world in which nothing made sense. Time seemed to stop. This quiet moment gave Will the chance to ask himself how he was going to tell Emma why he was there. Part of him wanted just to get up and leave.

He would have fulfilled his promise to find Emma and he could report back to Frederick that his daughter was alive and well. On the contrary, that couldn't be so – how could she be well in her present state as a drug addict? Would Frederick want to see her like this? There was no escaping the fact that he would have to tell her about her father's poor health and his continuing love for his daughter. He was in a quandary. The gentleman seemed to sense his anxieties.

"You appear confused, dear sir. All will be unfurled, if you wait. 'All in good time' as you English say, though the word good is not a word to which Time is applicable."

He sank back into quietness again. All this talk about time. It hardly seemed appropriate to a place where nothing appeared to be happening, except the smoking of opium, and in the kind of surroundings where you couldn't imagine anybody wanting to be.

Will felt the urge to wander about, rather than sit there on the edge of the bed, watching the others fall into a stupor. So he got up and walked back in the direction of the entrance area, intending to get some fresh air. On the way to the front door, he glanced around the small anteroom. His eyes being now well adjusted to the dark, he saw something he had not noticed when first he entered the dwelling.

In the corner, there was a baby's cot. Moving slowly forward, he glanced inside. His eyes widened with surprise on seeing a baby, quietly sleeping. It was slightly dark-skinned. Its age was perhaps three months. What was it doing here? Whose was it? He quickly realised it had to be Emma's. So yet another shock. The situation seemed hopeless. He could not see there being a happy ending to all that he was witnessing.

Wanting time to think, he went to the front door and opened it. Pretty soon, he closed it again. He felt safer back inside the house than looking out on the dismal blocks of buildings crammed on top of each other. He was so close to the window of a dwelling opposite, conversation would be easy without raising your voice. So he went back to the baby. It was beautiful, so calm and sleeping happily. He did not want to disturb it, so he went and sat down, crossed-legged on the floor near the cot.

Emma then came out of the bedroom. She picked up an old chair from a corner of the room and sat near Will. It was apparent she was now ready to talk, although she seemed nervous and excitable. She spoke quietly, leaning towards him.

"I have not seen you since those days of the strike. My God, that seems such an age ago. Goodness knows how you found me. I thought I had covered all my tracks. I never expected to be found by anyone from my past. I've become pretty good at becoming anonymous and moving on. Nobody in Limehouse knows my real name or much about me, except that I run this opium den. That's how I like it."

"Emma, I don't care how or why you came here. It's not my business. All I want to do is to tell you about your father. Please listen to me. After I've said what I have to say, it's up to you. I will probably walk out of the door and leave you in peace. So, may I carry on?"

"Alright, I'll listen," she said, in a very unconcerned manner. "Was she really so uncaring?", he thought.

"The first thing to say is that your father loves you."

"I don't think he'll love me as I am now."

"I would let him be the judge of that. He'll also be so happy that you're alive and not dead."

"Alive or dead? I'm not sure which would be better for me. Probably it were best if I was dead."

"That's rubbish talk. Now let me continue. If there's anyone who's near death, it's your father."

Emma reacted to that remark. "What's happened?"

"I have to tell you, Emma," Will said slowly, "that your father is a very sick man. He had an accident at work and got run over by an engine. It damaged his back and one of his lungs. He is not able to move about much, otherwise he would be the one searching for you, not me. He suffers from bouts of breathlessness and the great fear is that in any cold spell, he could easily die of pneumonia, be gone in a puff of smoke, as they say."

Emma lowered her head, clearly affected by this news. Just then, the baby stirred. Emma got up and cradled it in her arms. She was the mother then, as if there were any doubt.

245

"She needs feeding. I give her my milk, even though I know it's poisoned. Do you mind?"

"No..please..do you want me to leave?" Will asked.

"Not if you're not bothered." And with that she undid the front of her dress and lowered the baby's head to one of her breasts. Just like my Mary, thought Will, she was not embarrassed – it was a man's problem if he felt awkward.

Will continued talking. "Your father has become a very close friend of mine. He made it possible for me to educate myself through library books. I'll always be grateful for that. When he asked me to find you, I couldn't refuse him. He's a good man." He paused. "And he misses you so much – so does your mother and your brothers and sisters. They are all a great bunch of people."

"Please, Will, don't make me feel worse than I already do about what I have done to my family. But once I moved away and then got into trouble, I was too ashamed ever to return. I convinced myself they would never want me back – a fallen woman."

"Except that is where you are not right in what you're saying. Their love is greater than ever. They're sincere Christians who regard you as a lost sheep whom they want to find and welcome back into the fold. They would care for you, help you."

"Me, in my state? I'm beyond help."

"I don't know if you are or not. Mary, my wife, works at The London Hospital. I'm sure they've had to deal with opium takers."

"No, I don't think I can face that. Without my fix, I'm sure I'll fall apart."

"What about your baby? What's its name?"

"It's a she and I've called her Grace. The name expresses my wish for salvation for her, if not for me."

"You're being too hard on yourself."

"I'm an addict for opium, Will. That's serious."

"I know, but I'd like you not to give up on yourself. I know that's easy to say. I mean, I have to admit I've been addicted to alcohol. I'm trying to work on it now. Let's come back to your daughter Grace. How do you see things working out for her?"

"I don't know. That's the one thing I'm not sure about."

Just then a voice from the bedroom called out, "Why don't you two come back in here. You'll be more comfortable and we can talk together." There was something in that man's voice which suggested authority as well as strength. They obeyed.

"I've heard you called Will. My name is Thirkankara Chandragupta, but you can call me Adi for short."

"Pleased to meet you Adi," Will said in reply.

"By the way, Will, Adi is a prince in his home land," added Emma.

"Enough of that, my dear. I don't play that role while I'm here in Limehouse. I'd have trouble not only with the Lascar seamen but also with your friends the police. Given our trade here and given their prejudice against 'coloured persons' as they call us, they might accuse me

247

of disorderly conduct or some other offence they'll make up."

"That may be so," Will said, "yet it was a copper that helped me get here."

"Your sense of fairness does you credit Will. However, what intrigues me is why you have come on this mission."

"I think you've heard what I've said. It was to find Emma."

"That's also very noble of you, though I don't think we do many things in life without some sort of selfish motive. We don't remove the 'I want' from what we undertake."

"You're a clever fellow, Adi. If I'm honest, yes I had a reason. I've been drinking too much the last few years. I exhausted myself campaigning for the rights of the working man. And just when we think we're succeeding, we lose again. I needed time to think what to do next."

"What sort of campaigns?" asked the prince.

"A group of us want to take action against the old bosses who run our lives. We wanted a redistribution of power, to set up socialism and to work towards social justice for the working class."

"Goodness me! What an agenda. No wonder you're exhausted. You've been trying to act like gods, sweeping everything away with a magic wand."

"Don't you think a little more fairness in this world a good thing?"

"A good thing! What moral earnestness you possess.

Would you want to impose your ideas on others? Perhaps they don't want what you want."

"Isn't socialism a good thing?"

"There you go again – a good thing. Socialism is an abstraction. It's not living in the real world as people understand it. And all this talk of the poor inheriting the world one day – it isn't going to happen."

"Why not?" Will asked.

"You tell me. You say you're exhausted after failing to achieve this great goal of social justice. How did you and your friends fail?"

"Because we can't easily persuade the workers to put into government people of their own kind. We were able to march them half way up the hill but then found they wanted to run back down again. People get scared just when power could be in their grasp."

"So perhaps you expected it all to happen at once, this power. That change is irreversible, 'once and for all'. It's nonsense. You British for example probably imagine you will own India for ever. But we Indians are used to seeing empires come and go. It will be the same with the British one day.

"Let me tell you a story. There was once a proud king, known for his wrongful deeds and making unreasonable demands on his people. One day, a mysterious guest arrived, a young boy. He asked for and obtained an audience with the king. He was actually a god in disguise. The boy explained how universes come and go, without number and without time. While he was talking, a procession of ants made its appearance on the palace floor, moving in columns.

"The boy explained, 'Each ant was once a ruler, like you. Like you, each sought to act as a god. Now they have become reborn as ants'. As we Hindus understand it, the tale is a way of saying that one's wishes cannot be imposed unwillingly on others and that only individual acts of merit can lead to salvation."

"So you don't deny the advantage of trying to do good for others in this life?"

"Oh, come now. The point is that a man is answerable only to himself. Generally we live our lives trapped in a state of ignorance. Breakthrough is not easy, but once we realise our own limitations, we need to find something that is bigger than ourselves. The search for truth, for wisdom and for personal peace within oneself, can only come once we see ourselves as part of the process of Time – Time which is endless. Your life is a finite thing but time is infinite.

"You can't control events in time any more than you can control the movements of others. Your influence is limited and it is foolish to seek to impose change before others are aware of its benefits. People are naturally fearful of change. Your satisfaction must be within yourself in doing those things which bring you peace whilst working for the benefit of others."

After a pause, the prince added, "Now, my dear Emma, I think it's time for a smoke."

So the ritual began again. Meanwhile Will was

pondering on what the Prince had been saying. Time was indeed beyond anybody's ability to control, and the future was full of endless possibilities, with events and actions unforeseen or unimaginable. Yet there was also the chance of personal salvation through good deeds. Then he looked at Emma and realised how far she had come from being a match girl in Bow. Time and circumstance had certainly altered her but could she be saved?

Will then looked at Emma and Adi and said, "Prince Adi, if I can call you that, your words are powerful and have had an effect on me. However, I have to ask, how do you explain your present circumstances in this opium den? Surely, there is no salvation in smoking opium?"

"Ah, you have spotted my own personal weakness. The desire for this substance both clouds my thinking and gives me release at the same time. I can depart into imaginary worlds. I can feel calm and peaceful and relaxed. At the same time I know this is also an illusion. I am not seeking for the truth in myself, but escaping. My mind seems to be in control, though in fact it is not. Still, at least within these four walls, my dreams keep me safe from harm."

Will continued, "I have heard that during states of hallucination, a person can do daft things, such as imagining they can float whilst they jump off a bridge and kill themselves." He was looking at Emma when he made these remarks.

"Exactly," replied the prince, "that's why we smoke

in these safe surroundings. And we offer a service to others. As you saw earlier, everyone is welcome here – even your copper. And yourself. Anyone can drop by for a smoke and they leave what they wish to donate in the tin box on the small table behind you. We welcome all, without asking their race, religion or class. We have had people of quality come here as well as sailors wanting a quick smoke before boarding their ship."

"This can't be the road to wisdom – smoking opium. You're kidding yourself. It's an evil drug that is harming and destroying you," Will insisted.

"That's enough, Will," said Emma fiercely. "You're the one who's disturbing the peace now. Leave us to our pleasure."

"Emma, my dear, you know how I like to talk and debate," said Adi, "Our friend's words are not hurting me. The truth can only hurt if you're not prepared for it. My friend, I am like a chariot driver who has gone off the road. I let the reins of my mind get out of control. Luckily though, my senses which act as the horses, have allowed me to survive. So, there is help for me, as there is for all of us. However, I am under no illusion as to the fact that my deeds or karma have become such as to warrant many rebirths before I achieve my salvation. That is the nature of our philosophy."

"I don't want salvation, only some peace of mind," Will countered.

"Then I have told you of the road whereby you can attain it. Patience is what you lack."

And with that, he sank into his peaceful stupor, with Emma lying beside him, whilst she kept a wary eye on Will. He sat on the floor until he found himself falling asleep.

CHAPTER 20

Things Fall Apart

Later that day, Will woke to hear sounds coming from out of the back, past the bedroom. Through a curtain at the far side of the room, there was a kitchen area. Emma was obviously preparing some food.

When it was ready, Will, Emma and Adi sat at various points of the bed, eating some fish and potato and a kind of flavoured tea.

"The meal is delicious," said Will. "What's the unusual taste?"

"That is due to the addition of lemon grass," Adi informed him.

"Tell me more about the opium you smoke," said Will. "Do you buy the stuff in those small bottles or do you have to make it yourself?"

"We prepare it ourselves," replied Emma. "There's a skill in preparing opium. First, you have to know your supplier. I get ours from a long-established chemist near The London Hospital. The firm goes back a long way as a supplier of patent medicines. I deal with a particular member of the firm who knows me and who also knows I won't put up with rubbish. He sells me a quantity of raw opium. It costs about twelve shillings a pound. I like Persian opium the best, because it's the most pure, with no dirt in it. Mind you, in the past, I've had some poor stuff which was also Persian.

"The quality can only be determined once you've boiled the stuff in a clean copper vessel. There's one out the back. We pour off the water and strain the rest through canvas – there's plenty of that round the quays at Limehouse. Add a little of the scrapings from an old pipe and it should be ready."

"How much do you smoke each time you light up?" Will asked.

"About half an ounce, I'd say," Emma replied.

"Emma, by the way, is an expert in this field. She has a good business brain you know," chipped in the prince. "She runs the shop, as you say, keeping the customers happy with good quality dope and getting the money off them afterwards."

"Except," intervened Emma, "that these days the seamen have to be back on board their ships by seven pm, supposedly to stop them staying in places like this. We now have to rely on getting them to come in the mornings, instead of at night."

"But still they come," said the prince.

"Yes, perhaps," said Emma, "We used to get some right classy people. Now and again, we even managed to get them to sign a photograph of themselves, if we promised it would never leave these premises. There's one or two hanging up in the other room. But the baby seems to affect the customers these days – they tend to hurry through into this room."

This was the opening Will had been waiting for. "That brings us back to the question of the future of your baby. Why not let Grace be looked after by your mother or your sisters?" Will said. "Is this the best place for her to stay?"

His remarks further unsettled Emma. She knew this was an issue she could not avoid.

"I think I can manage," she said, not very convincingly.

Pleadingly, Will said, "Emma, I have to ask. Is there any chance of you coming back to West Ham, just for a short visit? You can discuss the baby's future with them. They can help you, maybe look after the baby."

"I can't, Will. I can't go without my regular fix. You don't know what you're asking. The journey, the anxiety – I'd panic. It's too far." There was desperation in her voice.

"I'll take care of you and Grace. Together we'll get there. It's only a few miles you know," Will suggested, in the hope of trying to change Emma's mind.

"But, after all that's happened, I can't, I can't." Emma started sobbing.

At this point, the prince stepped in. "Emma, don't drive yourself into a corner over this. Will is trying to offer his help. You would always have had to consider what would be best for our child. It is your duty to do so, as it is mine. We cannot evade the issue.

"May I suggest we invite Will to stay the night with us? In the morning, consider what is in your heart and what makes sense to your reason. Maybe all that's happened today was inevitable. Will has simply been the messenger from afar. He needs to know what he is going to tell your father when he leaves, or whether you will be accompanying him."

"And you won't mind me going and leaving you perhaps?" said Emma through her tears.

"What we have experienced together has been wonderful. We have known love and friendship in its most physical and spiritual sense. I respect you as a woman. I think that together we have been part of each other's liberation. But, that doesn't mean I can claim you or insist on keeping you against your will. We must always be prepared to move on, as fate intervenes in our lives."

Emma was very moved by these words. She said, "I will think on things and tomorrow we will decide. Will, are you happy to stay here? I can find a blanket or two, if you don't mind sleeping on the floor next door, with the baby for company?"

She almost giggled at the thought.

"That's fine," Will replied. "I can cope with a floor and baby Grace. It won't be the first time in either case."

That's how it was settled. With blankets to keep him warm, Will lay there until sleep came over him. His mind was full of the words the prince had uttered that day. He concluded that the prince was very educated and clever, a true aristocrat. It was just a pity about the dope, but then he wasn't the only one with a bad habit. The prince's might kill him but then so could alcohol with himself, if he wasn't careful. He also considered Emma had been lucky to meet the prince. He must have offered her a sense of security and protection after the break-up of her relationship with Alfred Haig.

They all woke up early with Grace crying to be fed. Emma came into the room to sort her out. After that, there was the 'winding' process – placing the baby over one shoulder – which Will offered to do. He loved the sensation of hugging a baby, regretting the fact that he had missed so much of this caring for a child while always out at work. Emma appeared relaxed this morning. Will wondered whether she had already had a smoke, but the usual smell was not coming from the inner room.

Emma went back into the bedroom. Will could hear softly-spoken words, followed by the sound of drawers being opened and closed. The sounds then transferred to the kitchen area – breakfast was being put together. It was to be a simple but welcome affair of bread and tea. Will sat on the edge of the bed to eat with them.

"Will," Emma said, "I am going to come with you. At the moment I'm only thinking of going there to see my parents and then coming back here. You'll have to be patient with me. If I feel the need for something to relax my nerves, you'll have to excuse me if I go off for a few minutes. I will take a small bottle of laudanum to keep me going until I get there and during the visit. Then I'll need some more to face the journey back. I'll carry Grace, of course, if you carry this small bag of mine. How do you propose we travel?"

Will replied, "We'll get a horse tram down East India Dock Road. Once we reach the Lea crossing, we'll have to walk. But it's not far. I'm sure we'll get there."

"Are my parents still in Tidal Basin?" she asked. Will nodded

Emma insisted she had to take time for a last smoke, Adi having done the preparation. Ten minutes later she emerged. She had put on a hat and tidied herself. Will could see she needed all her strength to undertake this trip. Her breathing was deep, but measured. Adi had got off the bed and all three now stood in the anteroom. Emma and Adi embraced. Will shook Adi's hand – it was the first 'coloured' man's hand that he had ever shaken. It was a firm grip, but not hard. The prince's eyes twinkled as he wished them good luck.

"I hope we meet again, if not in this life, maybe in the next rebirth," Adi said. "We can compare notes on how our deeds or karma have been recorded, whether good conduct will return us as human beings or damned to a lower life form for our sinful actions. However I think you'll be moving upwards," he said with a gentle laugh.

The door was opened and the three of them left. It

soon became apparent that Emma felt much more confident than Will in this area of London. She was known and greeted by those they passed on the street. "How's the baby?" and "Good to see you out, looking so posh," – things like that. Will noticed how much she was shown respect. Will sensed this was going to be an important journey for her. She was working hard to keep herself together. He felt responsible for the welfare of both mother and child.

Things started well. They got the tram going eastwards. The baby was superbly well-behaved. Emma appeared nervous but calm. But it did not last.

They had not gone more than half a mile, when Emma got up and screamed, "I've got to get off. Let me off! Let me off!" Such a commotion alarmed all the other passengers. Emma got up and rushed to the back of the vehicle. Will thought she was about to jump off from the tram platform whilst it was moving, but the driver saw what was happening and quickly reined in the horses to bring the tram to a stop.

Emma jumped off, clutching the baby, with Will quickly following. She then nearly got run over by a cab, which also managed to stop suddenly. Emma reached the pavement and sank down on her knees, crying, "I can't do it. I can't do it. I need my bottle, or I'll kill myself."

Will rummaged in her bag, found her bottle and let her swig down some laudanum. Her face was flushed and she was breathing heavily. Will was in a panic, aware they were creating a scene. People started to come up to them. Will was determined that Emma was not going to make a spectacle of herself. He gripped her firmly by the arm and said, "You're coming with me, whether you like it or not."

Will stepped back towards the edge of the road and shouted to a cab to stop. To his surprise, the driver did. "Emergency," Will said, "Emergency, please driver, would you take us to the London Hospital?" He looked at the three of them, not sure what to make of the situation.

"Alright," he eventually said, "Hop in."

He drove fast and got them there in under fifteen minutes. "Don't suppose you've got any money, have yer? For the fare?"

Will pleaded, "Driver, I've got some pennies, would you take that? I'm sorry it's all we have."

"In that case, get along with you. Get that young lady sorted out, whatever's the matter with her." This was to be Will's one and only ride in a Hansom cab.

Will thanked the driver before cajoling Emma up the hospital steps. She did not seem to understand what was happening to her. Will pushed her through the doors of the hospital. He was desperately hoping Mary was on duty. Luckily she was. Will waved frantically. Mary responded by coming over to them, once she had given instructions to other staff at the desk.

"It's Emma Horth," Will said, "I think she's in a mess."

Mary sized up the situation, before indicating they

should move to the front for further questioning. "It's the opium," said Will.

"She's probably suffering from some sort of panic attack. Is the baby hers?"

"Yes, it's hers, only three months old, I think."

"She'll need attention too. Wait here a moment."

Emma began to sob uncontrollably. She had used up all her strength getting this far. A few minutes later, a nurse came up to them.

"You're going to be admitted for observation, you and your baby. Come with me. I just need to ask a few questions." Emma, who by this time had calmed down, offered no resistance. With the nurse gently holding her arm, Emma moved off down a corridor casting a glance behind her in Will's direction before vanishing into a room. Will left the hospital, after checking when it would first be possible to visit her. He was anxious to see Frederick Horth and the family with the news.

As Will approached their house, he was spotted. Shouts of, "It's Will, he's back," were heard from the Horth children. Jane, Frederick's wife, opened the door and greeted him. Such excitement there was when he gave them the news. They were overcome with joy. Endless questions were piled upon Will – "How is she?" "How did you find her?" "Will she come back home?" Will had to answer apologetically that he could not say.

Frederick himself looked closely at Will. His head nodded as if to say, "Thank you." He did not speak at all until he said, "I want to see my daughter. When can I do so?"

Will told him about the hospital visiting hours. Frederick turned to Jane, and said, "I want to go to the hospital, at two o'clock sharp the day after tomorrow."

"How are you going to get there, Dad?" asked his daughter, Joan.

"I will walk there, if need be, starting now to make sure I get there on time."

"Frederick, that'll not be necessary," Will said. "I'll speak to my old mate Joe and see if we can't find a spare horse and cart somewhere which we could use. Don't worry. We'll get you there."

Two days later, Frederick was all ready for his journey when Will turned up outside the door with the horse and cart. Frederick had put on a clean shirt and tried as best he could to look smart. Using his walking sticks, he moved slowly towards the cart. He was going to be accompanied by his wife and one of his daughters. The rest of the family had to be persuaded to stay at home. "They won't allow many visitors at a time," their mother insisted.

Will announced, "Not much comfort here I'm afraid. There are no seats so we had to get hold of a few bales of hay in order to make a support for your back, with a couple of other bales on each side to prevent you moving about from side to side."

Frederick got in the back and slowly shuffled himself

backwards until he reached the bale placed there for his back. The others clambered aboard and off they went. When they reached the hospital, Frederick was helped out of the cart. Taking his wife's hand, he slowly climbed the steps into the hospital, breathing with difficulty. Will found out where the patient was being kept. An upright trolley was placed at their disposal to move Frederick to the ward. Will had never been this far inside the hospital before. The sheer size of the place amazed him.

When they got to the ward, they were met by the sister. "No excitement, please. The patient is undergoing treatment and must not be alarmed."

Mary, always with a splendid sense of timing, had arrived on the scene and stood in the wings as Frederick was ushered towards Emma's bed. The next thing that took place could only be described as extraordinary. In spite of the pain in his back and his other infirmities, he stood up, only to sink down onto his knees by the side of the bed.

Putting his hands together, as though in prayer, he exclaimed, "My Lord, blessed art thou for having restored my daughter to me. Truly the lost sheep has been found. I am ready to go now, oh Lord, for my deepest wish has been fulfilled. Take me now, oh Lord, I am ready to depart this life in peace, rejoicing and calling thy name, my saviour and my keeper."

He lowered his head whilst clutching one of Emma's hands. He was sobbing uncontrollably. Will had never before experienced his friend in such an emotional state. All about were overcome with tears, except the sister.

"Now, we can't have you making an exhibition of yourself. Get up and please be quiet. You're disturbing the ward."

At that moment Mary came alongside the sister and said, "Excuse me intruding, sister. I happen to know this family. May I help him get off his knees? He might hurt himself if he tries to get up by himself. May I find him a chair? I'm sure he'll calm down quickly. He'll be no trouble."

At this moment, Emma who had been unconscious, opened her eyes. She saw her father on his knees before her. She stroked his hand and said quietly, "Forgive me, Father, for having disgraced you." She began to cry and moan out loud. Her father burst into a further flood of tears.

By now a chair had been found. Frederick was coaxed into sitting down but he would not let go of Emma's hand. He gradually quietened down whilst looking straight at his daughter's face.

Will reckoned it was time to leave the family to enjoy their reunion. Before he left the ward, he managed a quick word with Mary. "Where's the baby?" he asked.

"In a special ward. She'll be looked after until the doctors have decided if it would be appropriate to reunite her with the mother. But that also depends on how Emma responds to treatment."

CHAPTER 21

Reconciliations

It took The London Hospital just three weeks of treatment to get the opium out of Emma's system. With many members of the Horth family wanting to visit Emma, Will had to arrange with Frederick when he could go without overcrowding the bedside area. One day, before he was due to visit, Will told Frank, who asked whether he could accompany his father to the hospital.

"Dad, what sort of person is she now?" he asked. "I mean, is she just wild and uncontrollable, impossible to talk to? Is she angry or bitter about what's happened to her? Or is she broken and depressed and not wanting help from anybody? Or what?"

"So many questions," Will replied, "I really can't answer any of them, except to say that I think, deep down, she's a good person who's gone off the rails a bit, maybe mixed in the wrong company, but I don't know."

"I wondered whether she regretted leaving her old life and was wanting to go back to Limehouse," Frank continued. "She perhaps had a kind of settled life there, running her own opium den, rather than being cooped up in a hospital and experiencing all these withdrawal pains."

"Yes, but you know why she had to leave," said Will. "It was for the baby's sake. Emma realised that she either had to give up the baby or come away with her to see her father. But she thought it would be a quick visit to Frederick's and then back to Limehouse.

"If she hadn't had a turn on the bus, she might have got away with it although it would not have been a real solution for her or the baby. And there's another point to consider – I think the opium could well have ruined her health and killed her in the end."

"Do you think she'll get over her addiction?" asked Frank.

"I don't know the answer to that either. Your mother says it only happens sometimes that an addict manages to kick the habit fully. It's too tempting to slip back, knowing it's still legal to get hold of the stuff."

"And what about the prince fellow you mentioned?" asked Frank. "Won't he want her back with him? And in any case, does he know where to find her?"

"I've been thinking about that as well. I was wondering whether someone ought to write him a note telling him where she is. He is also, of course, the baby Grace's father. I reckon we'll see what Frederick Horth thinks about this, as well as Emma herself. You know, it's funny – us sitting here talking about Emma. She's not our problem and none of this need concern us anymore."

"Well, you went through enough trouble to find her and bring her back. It's not surprising you still feel just a little bit involved," said Frank.

"Well, that's as may be," was Will's rather limp reply.

"I think I'd like to join you when you next go to the hospital, if that's alright," said Frank.

"No, I don't mind if it's O.K. with the family. Why do you want to see Emma then?"

"Well, I have known her since we were kids. I just want to see Emma again after all these years, particularly since she's had such a tough and adventurous time, unlike mine perhaps."

When Will and Frank arrived at Emma's bedside, she was awake and surprisingly calm. She still had a thin and slightly haggard look but the effects of eating a regular diet showed. Her baby was there beside her mother's bed, sleeping soundly.

"Hello Will," said Emma, "and who have you got with you today?"

"Hello Emma," Will replied. "Do you remember my son Frank?"

"We played together as kids. I'm pleased to see you again, after all these years," Frank said, as he offered his hand as a greeting. He then stumbled out the words, "A..are you well today?"

"Yes, thank you Frank," Emma replied slowly, before adding, "My, you do look a lot like your father."

"How's that?" said Frank.

"You're both tall, somewhat lean, with a gentle manner. And both handsome, of course." Emma said that with a cheeky smile on her face. What a lovely smile it was.

"You're obviously a lot better, Emma," Will said.

"Well, I don't feel sick anymore when I try to eat. And the attacks of itchiness come and go a lot." Just then, she let out a great yawn. "Oh, excuse me, that's another thing I do a lot – yawn."

"So are you managing to come off the opium completely?" asked Frank.

"The doctors decided to try to get me off the drug quickly," Emma replied. "At first, knowing I would miss my daily fix, they injected me with full strength morphine. After the first day, they gradually replaced the morphine with quantities of boiled water. They put a needle in my arm with some substance that calmed me down and sent me to sleep. When I eventually woke up, the nurses informed me I had been through a period when I was delirious, anxious and in a panic. I was also told I was swearing, cursing and crying so much and causing such a disturbance that they put me in a separate room. Then I remember my body starting to tremble and shake, all my muscles began to ache. I was breaking out into cold sweats and constantly restless. Yet amazingly the craving for my fix was gone.

"The nurses here are marvellous. They give me daily massages and hot baths while doing their best to make me drink plenty of liquids and to start eating properly.

This wasn't easy when I felt nauseous. Now I've got less pain, I'm finding my skin feels incredibly itchy. They have even had to restrain me from tearing at my own skin. So, at this point in time, I have to say I am a lot calmer and not missing opium.

"The hospital has made it clear that under no circumstances should I return to my old haunts. The doctors will only discharge me when they are confident that I have found a secure home and one that can cope with the situation. Then they will be ready to let me out of here. That depends on my mother and father being able to put me up at home. They said they'd find room, whatever happens, though they're a bit full up with my younger sisters."

"You won't be going back to Limehouse then?" asked Frank.

"You know about that as well, do you? No, Frank, I don't want that. I know that now."

"What about, Adi, the prince, does he know that?" Will asked.

"Not yet. I will get round to sending him a letter sooner or later. He'll be alright. Though he was kind to me and our daughter. The only thing that might worry him is how to carry on the business. I was the brains there. Still, he'll find a way round getting a new partner or simply go back to India."

Will could sense Frank wanted to say something more, but nothing came out of his mouth. He decided to hold in his thought. Emma then let out another huge yawn. It was obvious she was tired and sleepy, so they excused themselves.

"I hope I see you again soon," were Frank's last words before they left.

"What's going on?" Will thought to himself.

Eight days later the London discharged Emma, in the firm hope that with the support from her family, she would continue her recovery. Not only was her diet a strict one, but she was to be kept under supervision. Most addicts, the hospital felt, could quickly go back to their old ways, unless checked.

Emma returned to her parents' house in Charlotte Street. Grace had been declared undamaged by her mother's drug addiction. Emma restarted feeding her while her mother looked after her the rest of the time. Emma's parents were constantly worried that their daughter would try to escape, but Emma never gave a hint of doing that. She seemed content to be at home, often holding Frederick's hand as a gesture of mutual support, as he sat in his own comfy chair.

What everybody wanted to know, of course, was her story – what had she been up to for so many years? Eventually she agreed to tell it and requested that Will and Frank be there to listen to her as well as the family. So, one evening, everybody was assembled in the Horths' small front room. Frederick's young children – Bessie and another Frederick – were allowed to sit on the floor and told to keep quiet.

Emma commenced with the words, "Let me say at the start, that by and large, I have only been able to get through the past ten years through the help of several kind people, though I was not always appreciative of that help and wasn't an easy person to live with. I was, and am, very independently-minded and like my own way. However, it's hard making your own way in life, especially as a woman.

"I know you must have thought me foolish and stupid for leaving home and going to Bow when only fourteen years old, but I felt I had to do it. You were crowded at home. I thought I could go and get a job, however rotten it was, and show I could cope.

"So I went and got a job at the match factory. Believe you me, all the horrible things you heard about working there were more than true. The spirit of the girls there was amazing. Then along came Annie Besant who inspired us to fight back against our mean and cruel bosses. It was probably then that I realised how much it was necessary for women to stand up for themselves or continue to be exploited and to be paid less than men. It had to be our fight, without men interfering.

"As you know, we won and it was great. But during the strike we had little food. I couldn't pay my rent and was thrown out of my digs. I was homeless, cold and hungry. So there I was, at the clothes market in Roman Road one day, looking around a stall selling shawls and feeling I needed a little warmth, to cheer me up. There was one shawl which as soon as I put it around my neck felt so smooth. I really wanted that shawl.

"I asked the stall-holder if I could have it on tick and I would get the money soon to pay for it (I wasn't sure how). He refused. I pleaded and still he said no, a little louder each time. I got obstinate and refused to take it off. By now, he and I were being noticed, what with the shouting. I wasn't trying to run away.

"Then, just at that moment, from behind me, a copper grabbed my shoulder and held me fast. The stallholder said I was trying to run off with the shawl without paying. I was accused of being a common thief. Well, that was it. I was charged with trying to steal a shawl and of being caught in the act. I was arrested, put in jail and brought before the beak. After a trial lasting a couple of minutes, I was convicted. To set an example to others, as they say. I was sent to prison for fourteen days.

"Prison was downright nasty and cruel. Women who committed a crime were seen as more deserving of harsh treatment than men. I was a condemned woman. I was so miserable. I felt my chances of returning home were now nil. So after doing my time on heavy physical work, like stone-breaking, I came out feeling a fugitive, unloved and unwelcome everywhere. The only company I could expect would be the drunks and prostitutes of East London.

"Luckily, it didn't quite turn out like that. Fate took a hand. One day, I ran into this man whose name I found out was Alfred. He said he'd seen me before in a dive of a pub where I used to do a bit of singing, to earn a few pennies and hope people would buy me drinks. But it wasn't enough to earn my keep. Anyway, he bumped into me on this street corner. I had a basket with me and in the collision, the contents fell out on the pavement – a few scraps of old bread."

'Life's hard then,' he said. 'Here, don't I know you from the Prince of Wales? You sing a bit.' I nodded and then asked him if he would give me a halfpenny for a cup of tea. He said alright and we went to a teahouse. I sat with him while he had one too. To me, he was fun to be with.

"We got on well and he began to ask me about myself. As you can imagine I felt uncomfortable with the situation and got up to leave as soon as I could. As I walked away, he came after me, wanting to know if I wanted a few hours of work with a chap he knew who employed girls in his factory making fancy, cheap umbrellas. I said I'd think about it and hurried off. I appreciated he was trying to help me."

Emma's father interrupted to say, "Emma, Will has met Alfred. We now know quite a bit about you and him. It seems he did try and look after you. For that, I am grateful to him."

Emma's mother then put a couple of questions to her daughter. "What I want to know is how you ended up in the workhouse for drunk and disorderly conduct. Was that anything to do with taking drugs as well?"

"Mother, if you work in a pub, chances are you'll drink

more than's good for you. I did not have a settled place to live and I didn't eat much. I was just sixteen years old and feeling unsure of myself in certain situations. I got angry easily. And if you get drunk and the police come after you and you haven't got a man to speak up for you, they come down hard on you. If pushed around, I would shout and struggle. I was forcibly removed from the pub and taken down to the workhouse. Perhaps they thought that would calm me down and keep me out of further trouble.

"Then the master of the workhouse felt it would be a good idea to try and sedate me. It was the so-called doctor there who first put me on laudanum. At first it made me sick but it did make me less aggressive. So, to keep me quiet, I had another dose which worked on me and I kind of enjoyed it. Then I took to playing up and being a nuisance so as to get another dose.

"It doesn't take long to become addicted. So when Alfred got me out of the workhouse, I needed money to buy this liquid stuff from a chemist. You only had to say you wanted a painkiller. It wasn't difficult.

"I went back to my old ways yet was conscious of the workhouse in Mile End as a supply source when I got desperate. So I created a scene to try and get back, smashing windows. That worked in a funny way but again, as I assume you know, Alfred came and got me out again. It was all rather crazy.

"Then I reached the stage when laudanum wasn't strong enough. It didn't give me a big enough kick to keep me going in the periods between doses."

Will felt compelled to intervene. "What was going on in your head, Emma, that made you suicidal?"

"Overdosing," replied Emma coolly. "It's as easy to take too little as to take too much. When I took too much, I went into a kind of hallucination. I would imagine such mad thoughts, many of them evil and destructive and I would not know what I was doing.

"I didn't really want to kill myself, except when I was coming down from an overdose, feeling such a mess and thinking I no longer deserved to live. But even after a couple of such dreadful experiences, you are still hooked and only wanting to live for your next fix which you know is quietly destroying you. Only thing you can learn is how and when not to overdose yourself.

"During the better moments between fixes, sometimes I could feel confident again. On those occasions I was determined not to give up on myself. I knew I was addicted to opium although I was not stupid. I could entertain people and, believe it or not, I could get to look after money. I knew men liked me and I came to feel I could handle them. One thing I did know was that I didn't want to be a prostitute.

"After the break-up with Alfred, I drifted – not down to Limehouse as I told him I would, but to the West End. I found a dosshouse to stay in at Covent Garden which charged four-pence a night. The houses there were pokey and unclean, yet, funnily enough, every window ledge had a flower box on it. However it didn't take me long to realise I didn't want to be a flower girl. Too much out in the open all day, in all weathers.

"I moved on down towards Cambridge Circus and Drury Lane. That was rough too – brothels everywhere and plenty of criminals. While I was in the district, a copper had his throat cut. Where I could, I got work singing in pubs. I used to dress fancy but woe betide any man who took me for an easy…what shall I call it in front of children… touch.

"I felt I could handle myself, with a regular fix to keep me going. I then started to appreciate that some of the women who worked as prostitutes in the West End were no fools. They'd get their money, working their daily shifts – ten am to eight pm or six pm to the early hours – but they'd keep the money, not have a ponce take it off them. They used the cash to open restaurants and shops and became respectable. They were both tough and clever girls in my book.

"In the West End you meet plenty of foreigners and show-offs. The more a man dressed himself up in immaculate outfits, with hats, boots and umbrellas, the more likely he was to be a fraud. I wanted to meet a real gentleman, if I could find one, and see what they were like, so next I went to the Haymarket and St James's.

"What a different world that was. Town and country came together in posh shops which sold outfits for the class of people who liked riding and shooting, with their hamper baskets. Down side streets, called mews, there were the livery stables. There were florists, fancy barbers, pipe and tobacconists, gentlemen's clubs, restaurants and hotels. Some of these premises even had electric lights and fittings, or so they said. Hansom cabs moved back and forth constantly.

"Although my clothes were a bit shabby all the time I felt I had as much right to be there as any gent. Then I came across a massage parlour and escort agency. I knew this could be risky but I wanted the chance to meet some of these gents closer-to. It may sound conceited, but I was trying to measure myself against them and see if I could put on as good an act as theirs. So I got a job – not sure how – perhaps because of my knowledge of London, my past experience as an entertainer, or just because they liked my personality.

"I hadn't worked there long when I met the prince – Adi – the man you met, Will. He had arrived in London for the Queen's Jubilee Indian Exhibition at Earls Court. He was staying at the Star and Garter Hotel, Richmond, where lots of Indian guests were staying. Wanting relief from endless receptions and hoping to get more involved in London life, he contacted my escort agency.

"He turned out to be good company, charming and sophisticated, very well educated and rich. He opened my mind to all sorts of ideas. He respected me and did not try to exploit me. It also didn't take long before I realised that he was as fond of opium as I was. 'Gift of the British Empire', he used to call it. We also both quickly saw a business opportunity in setting up a place in Limehouse because it was known to be the haunt of sailors and their like from around the world."

"Did you fall in love with this prince, Emma?" asked her mother.

"Not sure how to answer that – obviously we had a relationship and I respected him – yet I did not feel towards him as someone in love."

"Will you go back to him?" asked mother.

"No, mum. I think I've had my wild times. I've been foolish but I'm a different person now as a result of what I've been through. I'm pretty tough, you know."

"You've always been a handful," said her mother with a slight sigh.

"I want to say something," said Frederick. "You have put your mother and I through a great deal of worry."

"Yes, I know, I'm sorry," interrupted Emma.

Frederick continued, "And you're probably very lucky to have survived it all. You have undoubtedly learnt a lot. I can see you're still going to be a handful but at least you have kept your spirit and strength and as far as I can see, you are still at heart a good person. I am glad you have come back home and it is really good to have you with us."

Emma quickly moved across to her dad and embraced him. "Thanks Dad, and Mum. I will do my best to look after you now."

The sounds of the baby Grace upstairs brought the proceedings to an end as Emma, followed by her younger sisters, went to attend to her daughter's needs.

As Will and Frank came away from the house, Frank said, "I really admire that woman. She's tried to live her life independently, without completely ruining herself along the way."

"I agree with you, Frank," Will said. "Much of what she has been saying sounded similar to my journey from ignorance to greater understanding of myself and others. Along the way, I took to drink, she took to opium. What's the difference, as long as it doesn't kill you and you eventually manage to get on top of your addiction?"

"Do you think she's shown herself strong enough to kick the opium habit?"

"I hope so, Frank," Will said, "I really hope so."

Frank became more and more preoccupied in his head with thoughts of Emma. He went round to see her regularly. She liked him and listened to him when he spoke of wanting to give up the factory job and study to become a teacher. She had the effect of doubling his determination to extend himself beyond what he was doing. He needed someone to support him in taking risks, just like his parents had always supported each other and had given each other strength.

Frank and Emma became closer and perhaps to the surprise of many, but not his father, they eventually declared their love for each other.

It was Frederick who insisted on a proper church wedding. And only one church would do – the 'Cathedral of the East End,' as they called St Luke's. This was one church and one church event Will couldn't get out of. Frederick booked the church and a suitable date arranged so all the families, Walton and Horth, could attend. Most important for Will, he was back amongst his brothers and sisters.

On 16th December 1899, roughly three years after Will had found Emma in Limehouse, she and Frank got married. That day Will was a happy and proud father, feeling sure the marriage was going to be a long-lasting one. During the ceremony, casting his eyes about him, he found himself admiring the building, especially its great height and fine brickwork. He considered the superb colourful mosaics behind the altar with their gold leaf surround to be one of the most beautiful sights he had ever seen.

One final piece of the jigsaw fell into place when Will heard from Alfred Haig. Will had sent John Haig a letter informing him that Emma had been found alive and well. John Haig had passed the news on to Alfred. Alfred had then taken upon himself to enquire further as to Emma's health and on being told by Will of her impending marriage, he sent her a card expressing his best wishes for the wedding. Emma was touched by this. No more would there be animosity between the families – the Horths, the Waltons and the Haigs were at peace with each other.

Through error we come to the truth! I am a man because I err! To go wrong in one's own way is better than to go right in someone else's.

FM Dostoyevsky, "Crime and Punishment"

EPILOGUE

Will was looking round the bare walls and floors of the house he had occupied for nearly forty years in Charlotte Street. The wallpaper was faded and merely looked a pale green and brown. The curtains had long ceased to have any discernible pattern to them and the front windows always looked grimy from the amount of dust and dirt in the atmosphere outside.

His mind was full of yesterday evening when the family and their close friends had assembled for probably the last time. The year was 1908.

As he lifted the last piece of furniture – an old wooden chair he had inherited from his mother – he knew life would never be the same.

He turned towards the door of the parlour. Mary was coming through with a box full of pots and pans and a few china cups. "I think this is all, Will."

"It's going to be hard leaving Tidal Basin, after all these years, Mary" he sighed.

They passed into the street. Joe Badman was there with the horse and cart, borrowed from his work for a couple of hours.

"The horses will be relieved to be pulling people for a change instead of coal," he remarked, "I found some old hay to lay across the floor for you two to sit on during the journey."

Looking round, a few people had gathered in the street to see Will and Mary off. Many were out of work. The docks were witnessing a big decline in trade, the shipyards were gone and only the lucky ones found work in the warehouses and factories. People kept their sense of humour but times were not good for the folks of West Ham. In spite of high unemployment, especially in the docks, Will was fortunate. Through trade union contacts at the Town Hall, he was offered the chance to become the school caretaker at Stock Street School in Plaistow. Being tied accommodation, it meant he had to leave Tidal Basin.

Walter Horth was joking about things as usual. "Now Will, remember we'll let you come back to visit us, as long as you don't wear that fancy outfit and top hat they're giving you in your new job. We don't want no posh-looking types round here. No one will talk to you if you dress like a toff. It's bad enough you're moving to the lah-di-da district of Plaistow. I'm telling you, if we catch you putting on any fancy airs and graces, we'll send you right back where you've come from."

Will smiled. "Fat chance of that, Walter. I'll only look smart-like on the outside. All the rest of me will remain the same. And when I've departed this life, they'll still find the words 'Tidal Basin' printed somewhere on my head. You can't see it now because of the few hairs I've got, but it's there."

"Yes, I know that, Will," replied Walter, "but just make sure you don't forget us."

Joe intervened. "Now, come on you two, chatting away like old codgers. I told the foreman he'd have his cart back by noon."

Will and Mary got into the cart. As it pulled away, waves and 'byes' rang out until the corner of the street was turned.

The position of caretaker gave Will some security in his later years. He even began to wonder if he could reach the ripe old age of seventy when he could get one of the new old age pensions they were thinking about introducing. "Mind you," he said to Mary, "I'd have to be of good character and not a drunkard. But I think that's all behind me."

Now and again, Will made trips out to Essex and the places where his ancestors had lived. He felt it was important to remember them and what they had contributed in shaping the kind of person he was.

Mary had become a senior nurse at the London Hospital. She had declared she would retire soon. She hadn't made up her mind about getting married, though she did offer Will some hope that once she had retired, she would give the idea serious consideration. "One day, maybe I will, if you play your cards right." That playful look was still there in the eyes which had captivated Will many years earlier.

Frank had successfully applied for a vacant pupil-teacher post in West Ham and was on his way to achieving his goal. The money Will's mother had passed on to her children was finally put to good use for fees and examinations. He was told it could take up to eight years before he would be qualified.

Emma became a tower of strength in the suffragette movement. She got involved with the Bow Radical Group who realised her ability to involve people and organise petitions. One day it must come – votes for women.

Frank and Emma already had a son, David, with another due within the next few months.

When Will thought about those closest and dearest to him, they were a rebellious bunch – Mary, Emma, himself and Frank to some extent. None was good at complying with what was expected of their class and background. Even Will's dad had been a rebel in his own twisted way.

In spite of his pain, Frederick Horth maintained his dignity until the end. He caught pneumonia in 1902 and died soon after, satisfied that he had done his best for his family and that they were united again. From him, Will had learnt that friendship was more important than causes.

Emma's old partner in Limehouse, the prince, didn't quite disappear off the scene. He did leave London but before he did so, he left instructions with a firm of solicitors in the City of London for his daughter to be provided with a private education, with all the necessary fees to be paid out of his account. Grace was a lucky girl but it was the hope of everybody, including her mother, that it wouldn't spoil her and make her assume the airs and graces of a lady. They didn't want her to forget she came from working class stock in London's east end, as well as from an Indian aristocrat.

Back in November 1898, Will had got excited when the people of West Ham had elected the first–ever administration in the country which called itself socialist. It had not lasted long due to a controversy concerning the 'Freethinker', a magazine which was anti-religious. Once the 'Freethinker' became available in public libraries, it provoked a campaign against the council led by the churches and the newspapers. In the 1900 local elections the socialists were defeated. Will had taken it better than might have been expected by those who knew him.

The words of the prince had not been lost on Will. He had come to realise that change would only come when the time was right. Everything can't be done at once. "What's important is for people to stick together and not run away from their responsibility to help others," he said.

"The poor will always survive because the rich and the powerful need an underclass to serve their needs. The poor will accept the situation as long as homes and jobs are made available, as well as clean water. But they will always have to fight if they want to change things. It's never going to be easy. Never quit, whatever life throws at you."

ACKNOWLEDGEMENTS

I have used the resources of a number of archives and libraries across East London as well as Essex Record Office. All were most helpful. Foremost in my thanks would be Newham Local History Archives for unfailing co-operation and friendliness. Other sources include historical books, articles and internet sites.

The novel would not have been accomplished without the support I have received from several individuals.

Firstly, I would like to thank my friend, Bill (Sid) Bailey for his perspicacious comments and constant attempts to make me more rigorous in pruning text to increase its impact.

Secondly, I would like to thank those who read previous drafts for their helpful comments.

Thirdly, I would like to thank Iain Griffin for voluntarily proof-reading the novel and for his encouragement in seeking its publication.

Fourthly there is the person who has been my constant source of inspiration during this project and the person who has forced me to be logical and systematic in my emotional thinking, more so than I ever thought possible of myself. I am referring to my wife, Anne.

c.Hamilton I Hay
January 2013